The Cathedral

The Cathedral

a Fable

For information about permissions, other works, and the author, visit *craigscunningham.com.*

This book is set in the typeface *Athelas* designed by Veronika Burian and Jose Scaglione.

Paperback ISBN: 978-1-967262-47-2

A Publication of *Canowan* | Waco, Texas

Produced in Partnership with *Tall Pine Books* | Warsaw, Indiana

| 1 24 24 03 23 20 |

Published in the United States of America

The Cathedral

A Fable

Craig Cunningham

PART I:

The Boy and The Traveler

PART II:

The Young Man and The Architect

PART III:

The Man and The Magician

PART IV:

The Old Man and The Angel

PART I

The Boy and The Traveler

His heart was at home in the desert.

As birds soared through the sky, or as fish darted through the sea, Adeo wandered the space between the mountains. He was woven into the vastness. The horizons spoke to him. The wind recognized his scent. The stones carried the echo of his songs. The sun called him friend and the stars above saw him grow from one season to the next.

Adeo understood that everything in the desert had a name and a soul.

Even the great mountains layered in the distance had names and souls. All things longed to be known by this truth and not by the falsehoods attributed to them by foolish men. In this way he loved them. They loved him, too.

They nurtured his imagination.

They moved in and out of his dreams.

While drifting off to sleep he often heard their voices saying, "I know who you are, and I know who you will become. I see you truly as you see me."

* * *

The first Spanish explorers to his homeland gave new names to the mountains. Most were forgotten or changed back to the names by which the people of the desert first knew them. But one name remained, and that was La Catedral. The people of the desert kept the name because they hoped it might break the curse hidden inside the mountain.

Long before Adeo's time, a tribe of desert people entered La Catedral to take shelter from a storm. The families crowded into the cavern and held one another close. The doorway to La Catedral collapsed and trapped them inside. The storm raged for three days. When it finally passed, the others in their tribe dug the doorway out to rescue them. They entered the strange mountain but found no bodies or bones. The people were gone, as if they had never existed. The mountain swallowed them. From that day forward no one entered La Catedral for fear of being consumed.

But many years later, a boy came along who loved the mountain.

He loved its shape.

He loved its name.

He loved its voice.

Adeo loved the mixture of fear and beauty awakened in his heart when he stood small at its base and looked up. He often ran his hands around the edges of the stone doorway. He longed to go inside and face the magic on his own.

"Are you still in there?" he asked, crouching at the entrance. "Say something to me."

He feared not the world because he did not recognize the world as dangerous. He only knew the patterns of the sun, the touch of his mother's lips against his forehead, the shapes made by clouds adrift, the rare and exciting scent of rain, the thump of horse hooves to signify his father's return after a long day of work.

* * *

Adeo's family had little.

They lived in an adobe dwelling exposed in the center of a valley, surrounded by a bowl of mountains. In the same way an animal might come along and find an empty cave, Adeo's family came along and found an empty house. They moved in. The previous owner was certainly dead or had managed to escape the land. Adeo liked their home. His mother did, too. She sang sweetly to his new baby sister while tending the cactus garden from which they harvested medicine and food.

By twilight the smoke of the cook fire could be seen from miles away.

For many families, that would have invited thieves and raiders, but Adeo's father was protected from such attacks. He trained racehorses for an Arabian trader named Abu Faras. Abu Faras was a powerful and severe man with a ranch on the other side of the mountain pass. Those who worked on his ranch had nothing to fear. If anyone stole from his workers, Abu Faras cut off their hands. If anyone harassed their families, he threw them off a cliff.

The price for his protection was unending poverty.

The workers made the trade out of necessity. Abu Faras paid them minimal wages and deducted exacting costs for any resources they used, down to how many times they filled their canteens with water. His horses ate and drank better than the men who cared for them.

Some nights Adeo stayed awake and listened to his father and mother speak softly in the quiet dark.

"But what else can I do?" his father asked. "There is nothing here for us."

"God will provide a way," she answered.

"He will find us and kill us."

"God will provide a way," she said again.

The desert, by its nature, was unforgiving and unsympathetic to the plight of survival. It treated people indiscriminately from a bush or a lion or a stone that had been resting in the same spot for a thousand years. All were welcomed but none were promised accommodation. Certainly, none were promised prosperity.

* * *

Each morning Adeo set out on a voyage to see how far he could travel and still make it home before dinner. If lost, the sun showed him the way. If the sun went down, the stars knew the way as well. He feared not the places he had not yet been and longed to meet them face to face.

One morning, Adeo heard a girl singing over the ridge.

He crept forward to avoid making any noise and came to a large boulder that looked down into the crevice below. Beneath him was a girl, close to his age. She was drawing pictures in the sand and talking to herself. Sometimes she stopped talking and began to sing. She had dark hair and was barefoot, like him, though he could see a pair of black boots tucked against the base of stone. She wore fine clothes and her hair was clean and pulled back into a single braid.

Her face was pretty but marked by a scar running like a jagged river across her cheek.

Adeo watched her. He was mesmerized by her movements, her silliness, her ability to float over the earth. She played and used different voices for whatever story was unfolding in her imagination.

"I know you're watching me," she said after some time. "You don't have to hide."

Adeo tucked behind the rock. His heart raced. He wanted to run away. He said nothing and hoped the words were part of the game she was playing. The girl emerged from behind the rock with her finger extended at Adeo's face.

"You!" she said.

He tripped and fell backwards. She laughed sweetly.

"Why are you watching me?" she asked.

"I'm sorry. Because I don't know you."

"What's your name?"

"Adeo."

"I'm Sufiya," she said. "Are you real?"

Adeo thought it to be an odd question. But he had the same question for her.

"Yes. Are you?"

She held up her hand. He pressed his hand against it.

At once he understood she was a creature as wild as he, as connected to the workings of the sun and the moon as he, as woven into the sand and the sky as he.

"What happened to your face?" Adeo asked.

"Oh," she said, and lightly touched the jagged line. The question embarrassed her. The softness of her cheek was broken by a harsh split of red skin. "When I was little, bad men took me. They hurt me to get money from my grandfather."

"I'm sorry," Adeo said.

"It's ok. I don't remember any of it. I was too young."

"Who is your grandfather?" Adeo asked.

"Abu Faras," she said. "Come on. Let's play."

She took his hand and led him into the crevice. She was like a fire, too dangerous to ignore, too dangerous to resist.

* * *

Adeo and Sufiya became friends.

He often found her in the recesses of the mountains. Sometimes the universe pointed them to one another. Other times, it didn't. They never met in the same places but rather came upon one another unexpectedly in the wildness of the desert lands. If ever he heard her singing, he made his way to her. If ever she smelled him on the back of the wind, she made her way to him.

"Where is she today?" Adeo asked The Sky.

"I cannot tell you," The Sky replied. "Today you must find her on your own."

"The desert is too big. She can be anywhere," Adeo said.

"You and she are bigger than the desert," said The Sky. "Don't you see?"

He moved through the mountains until far away, on another peak, he saw her shape against the dawn. She saw him, too.

Sufiya lifted her hand and waved, and he waved back.

* * *

"We need to go to town today," Adeo's father said one morning.

Adeo wished to explore the mountains and search for Sufiya, but he said, "Yes sir."

"Get ready. We need to be home before dark. The horses don't like traveling when the moon is gone."

They saddled the horses and brought enough water for the journey. Town was over half a day's ride at a steady pace. They visited once a month for rice, beans, and any necessities like medicine or knives. His father's blade recently broke sawing through the neckbone of a deer he was skinning. A reliable knife meant as much to their survival as anything. They had to use up the meager savings held in a box at his father's bedside to replace it. Today, they planned to buy food but also boots for his mother. Hers had worn through.

Adeo did not tell his father that his own boots needed replacing, too.

His feet had been growing over the last year and his toes were curled inside the end. When not around his father Adeo removed the boots and ran barefoot through the desert. The stones grew scalding hot in the middle of the day and he leapt from bush to bush, landing his feet in the smattering of shade.

Adeo did not like going to town.

Main Street ran narrowly between lines of buildings that looked as if they might fall over at any moment. He grew terrified that all the world was closing in on him, the noisy voices and the fast-walking men and the wagons endlessly loading and unloading. A man and a woman bumped into Adeo as he climbed off his horse. The couple pushed through swinging doors into a building from which many more loud voices came.

"We have to be quick," his father said. "I will get the boots. You get the food. You know the correct amounts?"

"Yes," said Adeo.

"I can trust you," his father said. "You're growing up, Adeo. You're becoming a man in your own right."

Adeo went to the familiar store at the end of the street. He purchased the exact amount of food to sustain them for the month. He came outside and waited on the porch holding the bags. Down the street he saw his father talking to a group of men who were gathered around the most magnificent horse Adeo had ever seen. The Horse was stark white. Even its mane was white. The Horse was lovely but still wild. If the man holding the rope let loose an inch, the beast tried to rip itself free and escape.

A man Adeo did not recognize encouraged his father to inspect the animal.

This man was dressed in a suit. He smoked a cigar. They spoke for a moment and shook hands.

Right then, Sufiya ran into the street. The man in fine clothing lifted her up lovingly and drew her near to The Horse. He said something to her. Sufiya smiled. She wore a wide-brimmed hat and a pink dress. She reached out and ran her fingers through The Horse's mane. The man then set her back on the ground.

She met eyes with Adeo.

He took a step forward. Sufiya shook her head, no, as if to warn him to stay back.

Her eyes held a fear he had not yet seen. She avoided looking at him from that moment on. Her grandfather loaded her into a carriage and she was carted away. Not once did she look back.

Adeo's father approached him and gripped his shoulders. He had an unusual excitement and spoke in a breathless whisper.

"Wait here. Don't move!"

Adeo's father went into the clothing shop next door and there he stayed for nearly an hour.

Finally, he came out.

"Did you get the boots?" Adeo asked.

His father opened the bag. Not only did he buy his mother boots, but he also bought her a new dress inlaid with small flowers. Adeo's eyes widened. His mother would be joyful but equally angry that so much money had been spent on her.

"Don't speak right now," his father said. "I will explain everything soon. Today is a good day. God has blessed us."

They mounted the horses and cut through an alley to avoid Main Street.

Once far enough from town his father pulled to a stop. Adeo did, too.

"That man you saw me talking to was Abu Faras. The horse you saw is the finest racehorse in all the world. There is no amount of money you or I could imagine that would be able to buy that horse," his father said. "Abu Faras has asked me to train it, for triple my current wages. He says of all the trainers, I am the one he trusts the most. We are free, Adeo.

Finally, we are free. Death is loosening its grip on us, little by little."

* * *

For the next few months, his father's sole focus was training The Horse.

He came home later and later in the evenings but usually with good reports of progress. Abu Faras wished to race The Horse on Christmas Day to impress his granddaughter, Sufiya. The Horse was to be a gift for her, and she would be the one to name it. Adeo never told his father that Sufiya was a friend to him, and they had spent a thousand years together in this realm and others accessible only through dreams and imagination. He loved hearing about The Horse, and how it was as fast as a bolt of lightning ripping through the night sky. He loved hearing about the sound of its breath. His father had been pushing The Horse harder and harder and was soon to test its top speed on the plains, as Abu Faras had instructed him to do.

Their fortunes had increased greatly. If a rope unraveled, they simply bought a new one. On Adeo's birthday, his father appeared with sweet candies to celebrate. They mended things long broken. Abu Faras even sent him home with leftovers from his own family's table. Sometimes while eating Adeo wondered if the food on his plate was earlier on Sufiya's plate. The hushed late-night conversations between his parents came to an end.

"Soon we will have saved enough to move closer to the ranch," his father said one night at dinner. "And I won't have to travel so far every day. You will see more and more of me."

"I'm glad to see more of you," Adeo said. "But I like it here."

His mother leaned over and squeezed him tight.

"You will like it better where we are going," his father said. "This is our way forward. We finally have a chance."

Adeo did not like the idea of moving. If they lived in a new place, the mountains would have new faces and new names. Still, he was proud of all his father had accomplished, and, like his mother, he enjoyed the luxury of living without hunger or fear.

* * *

One night, Adeo crouched in the valley waiting for his father to come home.

In time two horses appeared against the blue horizon. His father was on one.

Adeo did not recognize the other rider.

"I see you there, Adeo," his father called out.

Adeo stood up.

"Run ahead and tell your mother we have a guest tonight."

Adeo ran home while the horses walked at a slow pace. Their family rarely accommodated guests. If a traveler came by in the night, his parents never turned them away, so long as they appeared trustworthy. On those rare occasions, Adeo slept outside to open his own bed for the guest. He liked sleeping outside. No roof blocked the view of the circling stars.

He told his mother the news then waited until the door opened.

His father entered first and was followed by an old man wearing a moth-eaten hat. He had a ragged beard and wore a long wool jacket that almost touched the ground. The old man quickly removed the hat and placed it over his chest.

"I hate to impose," he said. "If it's trouble for you or your family, I'll be on my way."

"Please, eat and rest," his mother said. "Then be on your way tomorrow."

On his shoulder The Traveler carried a bag that appeared heavy.

"Take his bag," Adeo's mother said to him. "Offer him water. Hurry, Adeo."

The Traveler handed the bag to Adeo and met his eyes with a slight smile. In the old man's face were lines hard won from a lifetime spent exploring the corners of the earth.

"Feel free to look inside. There's treasure in there," The Traveler said.

Adeo peeked inside the bag to find a stack of books. He had seen books in town, but his family had never owned one except for a partial leaflet of the Gospel of John.

"You don't mind?" Adeo asked.

"I insist," The Traveler said. "I've come all this way for you to see them."

The adults ate at the table while Adeo sat in the corner turning through the books. Not only did they have long blocks of words, they also had a great many illustrations. One of the books was composed of strange visions of creatures in outer space and metal machines that flew through the stars. Another book categorized animals and plants from faraway lands. The third book had drawings of enormous buildings that looked much like the mountains surrounding them. This third book spoke to him, just as the mountains spoke to him.

The Traveler looked over.

"Those are cathedrals," he said. "You can find them all over Europe. They are churches, used for the worship of God. They provide peace and safety and hope to all who enter their doors. Many cathedrals are hundreds—even thousands—of years old and are still standing to this day."

Adeo thought the cathedrals looked like the brothers and sisters of mountains.

He wished to build one of these cathedrals right where their house stood. There he would welcome men like The Traveler and give them ample space for rest.

That night, Adeo struggled to sleep beneath the open sky.

Visions of the cathedrals filled his imagination. Perhaps those great structures of stone spoke the same language as the mountains and the moon. Perhaps he could find them one day and ask how they came to be.

"What's hidden in your heart tonight?" The Moon asked the boy.

"I don't know," Adeo said. "The voices are all speaking at once."

"Then you must find the voice that matters most," The Moon said.

Before dawn Adeo awoke to a rustling.

He looked up and saw The Traveler loading his meager belongings into a saddlebag. The old man met eyes with Adeo. He offered a gentle nod, and to the horizon he rode.

At the foot of his sleeping mat, Adeo found the book of cathedrals left behind as a gift.

* * *

Adeo next saw Sufiya in the spring after a night of heavy rain. Much time had passed since that day in town, when she warned him to stay away.

The sky led him to where she played in a creek now running with water for the first time in years. She looked older. Her countenance had changed, like a portion of her innocence had been traded away. She did not look up at him when she said, "Where have you been?"

"Looking for you," Adeo said. "Every day, for many days."

"I am here to be found."

"You were embarrassed by me," Adeo said. "I only wanted to say hello."

"I was not embarrassed. I was protecting you," she said.

Finally, Sufiya glanced up at him and her eyes held the same warning as they did in town. She was changed. He could not identify the reason why, but the girl who wandered the mountains was transforming into something else. The scar on her face seemed darker.

"I don't want you to meet him," she said. "My grandfather. I don't want him to know who you are or where you live. I don't want him to see your face or hear your voice. The people close to him get hurt. I want to protect you."

Adeo made his way down to the creek. He crouched across from her. She was searching the water for something.

"There is gold in here," she said. "You can take it and give it to your family and go anywhere in the world but here."

He had walked the mountains for many years and never came across anything resembling gold. Sufiya snatched a stone from beneath the water, inspected it, and tossed it aside.

"After big rains, the mountains offer gifts to those who love them. My great grandmother told me the old tribes grew rich in this way. That's why they aren't here anymore. They took their riches and went east."

"No, La Catedral swallowed them."

"That didn't happen," Sufiya said. "It's a ghost story for children. The story of the gold is true, though."

Adeo ran his hand through the creek. He watched the thick layer of dust swept off his skin. He sunk his arms in the water and brought it to his face.

"Have you ever looked inside La Catedral?"

Sufiya continued searching the water.

"One time. Almost."

"But you were too afraid?"

"Not afraid," she corrected.

"Did you hear the voice? What did it say to you?"

She did not answer him.

They searched the waters under the quiet sky. With their heads down they came face to face unexpectedly. Adeo stood straight and so did she. They had never been so close, so exposed to one another. He looked into her eyes as if seeing her for the first time. She was a desert creature. Like a shining rock or a long-dead carcass or an arrowhead from some extinguished civilization, he wished to inspect her. He wished to spend his day beside her. He wished to use his hands to touch her hair, to trace her shape, to wonder where she came from and where she was going.

"May I touch your scar?" he asked.

Sufiya instinctively reached up to protect herself.

"Yes," she said. "But be gentle."

Adeo lightly brushed his fingertip along the length of the scar. He felt the break of skin, the raised flesh.

"Can I kiss you?" he asked.

"Yes," she said.

He quickly pressed his lips to hers and just as quickly separated.

They said nothing of the kiss and went back to searching the creek for gold.

* * *

Adeo overlooked the valley below. He wanted to listen to the mountains and the moon. They asked him questions he found difficult to answer. But he liked where they pointed his mind, as if they were guiding him to ancient and long-buried things few people knew how to find. Once a month in its fullness the moon cast a glow upon the world below and from this perch Adeo could see the whole valley lit up in black and white.

At the far end of the great valley he saw a figure moving fast.

The dark blur shot across the desert floor. The rider looked to be his father, but he wondered why he was running at full speed. A pit filled Adeo's stomach. Something was wrong. He edged forward on the cliff and saw now that his father was being chased by a group of five men.

Adeo hurried to descend the mountain. He reached the ground and ran as fast as he could back home and there found his mother and baby sister standing outside.

"Where is he?" Adeo asked breathlessly.

"What's wrong?" she asked.

"He was running across the valley, coming this way. Others are chasing him."

"Gather your things," she said.

Adeo rushed inside and stuffed his belongings into a satchel. He looked over and saw the book of cathedrals given to him by The Traveler. It was heavy and unnecessary for survival but still he placed it in the bag and returned to the front door.

Just then they heard the hoofbeats approaching.

His father appeared out of the darkness and swung off his horse in one smooth motion.

"You must run," he said. "They're coming. Don't look back. Go!"

Adeo's father owned one small pistol. He removed the gun from its holster and made sure the chamber was loaded. His hands shook.

"What happened?" his mother asked.

"I was riding The Horse. Too fast. It stepped into a hole and broke its leg. Now it has no worth. But they are coming. They are coming to take the payment." He approached his wife and held her face tenderly. "You must ride. Ride as fast as you can until morning. And don't look back."

He kissed her forehead.

She nodded. He helped her on the horse and settled the baby in her lap.

Adeo's father looked at him.

"And you too," he said. "You must look after them."

"I will stay with you and fight," Adeo said.

His father gripped Adeo's arm and pulled him to the horse. "We have no time. Protect them. Go!"

As Adeo put his foot into the stirrup, the other horses and riders walked into the edge of the light created by the warm glow of the home. Their hardened faces showed no signs of mercy. The man at the front removed his pistol and held it across the saddle horn.

"There's nowhere for you to go," he said.

"The payment is mine to make," Adeo's father said. "And I will make it."

"The Horse was worth more than your life. Your blood alone is not enough to pay the debt."

"It was an accident."

"Accident or not, The Horse is gone."

"I will make a way."

"He has ordered it to be done."

At once Adeo heard the mysterious language he loved to speak. The Moon above said to him, "All will be ok. Even in death, all will be ok." He looked up as a cloud rolled in front of the moon and the ground below grew dark.

"Run," his father said quietly to his mother. He slapped the horse's haunch. The horse whinnied and rose on its hind legs.

His father drew the pistol and fired upon the man who was speaking. The bullet knocked him from his horse. His father fired again, now on the second man, to give her time to escape.

Gunshots filled the night.

Adeo scrambled to the edge of the house in search of a rock that he might be able to throw if someone came close enough. The sound was deafening, all the shooting. His hand gripped a rock and he threw it with all his strength in the direction of the men and knew not where it landed.

Two of the riders roared past him in chase of his mother and baby sister. They fired their guns at her. Adeo saw his mother fall into the sand. The moon saw it, too. All the mountains saw, too. She wore the pretty dress bought for her on the day he and his father went to town. The two riders came to a stop over where she and his baby sister lay still. They spoke to one another briefly then fired two more shots into the bodies.

They returned to his father's body curled in the sand. They unloaded one shot after another into him. They seemed to take pleasure in the killing. Adeo launched another rock and knocked one of the men from his horse. The others laughed. Two were dead, but they cared nothing for their friends just as they cared nothing for his mother, his father, his sister. They cared nothing for life itself. Adeo seized the reins of a loose horse and turned into the night and ran.

"Let him get a head start," someone shouted. "It'll be more fun to catch him."

Behind him Adeo heard more gunshots. The rush of wind spread his tears all the way back to his ears as the moon showed him the path forward to La Catedral.

Adeo dismounted the stolen horse and stood before the entrance to the mountain.

Many times, he had stood in this place, but never had he gone inside.

A gunshot kicked up dirt by his feet. He looked back and saw the three remaining men closing the distance between them.

The Moon said, "Go inside. You will be protected."

The boy slid through the opening and into the shelter of La Catedral. He felt his way to the cavern wall and sat down. He tucked his head between his knees and prayed with his eyes shut tight.

PART II

The Young Man and The Architect

Beyond the dark horizon was Africa.

Some days while staring over the waters he longed to keep going.

More often, he realized that he had gone far enough.

Adeo gazed past the ships in the port of Marseille, hazy in the still-dark morning. He liked the sound of fishermen grumbling that the world had changed. He liked the smell of their cigarette smoke in the cool, fall air. They often claimed the good days of fishing were behind them. They complained about the government. They hid their earnings. They spoke of tides and the shape of the moon. The oldest ones spoke the least. They had already said everything they needed to say. He liked this new variation of the language of men and knew enough French by now to make his way around the city.

Behind him a clocktower rang out. He wrapped up his breakfast of bread and butter and placed the leftovers inside his satchel. The remainder would serve as lunch, and if he was frugal, his dinner. Adeo walked north on the boulevard. Rising into the gray sky he saw the Cathédrale de La Major. In this light the church looked more like a mountain than a building and he felt a pang of longing for the home he had left behind so many years ago.

Adeo walked around the side of the building to a small entrance tucked within an alcove. He knocked on the door. A priest let him inside and guided him to the empty sanctuary. Adeo sat down at a pew and began to sort through the items in his satchel.

"Do you have enough light?" the priest asked.

"I do," said Adeo. "Thank you."

"May I see them again? The drawings?"

Adeo removed a notebook from his satchel. On the tattered pages were sketches of churches from across Europe and the details that made each one unique. He wrote notes about the sound of water. He patterned the movements of the sun and the moon through stained-glass windows. He discovered that the story within the glass changed from day to night and season to season. Christ crucified in the moonlight revealed a different truth than Christ crucified in the sunlight. By now he had lived in Cologne, Milan, Florence, London, Barcelona, and many other places that were home to the grandest cathedrals in all the world. He spent at least a year in each place. He arrived on the doorstep at dawn and told the first priest he encountered of his intentions to build a cathedral in the deserts of his homeland, then asked if he might be allowed to make sketches. He offered his hands as a broomsweep or a carpenter in exchange for access to the building. Few required payment. They pitied him, perhaps. Certainly, they considered him naïve. They saw him as an artist and a dreamer who knew little of the sacrifices required to bring a cathedral from mind to matter.

Adeo handed the notebook to the priest who angled the pages into the light of a candle. He slowly turned through the sketches.

"Westminster," the priest said. "I saw it once as a boy. I remember the sound of the bells. A beautiful place."

"Look there," Adeo said.

Drawn in the corner was a bell with the inscription 'Christe Audi Nos'.

"Christ hear us," the priest said. "May He hear us, indeed."

In time the priest handed the notebook back to Adeo and said, "You have a talent. That is certain. And a big dream. An impossible dream. But God works in the impossible."

The priest turned and faded into the darkness.

Adeo faced east. He wished to see the first rays of sunlight pressed against the glass, and then upon the floor. How might the light change the form of all it touched? How might the light awaken his own soul? Could light change matter from one thing to another?

"Show me what I need to see," Adeo said quietly to The Sun.

He waited for the response but only heard the shuffling of the priest's feet in the distance.

* * *

The priest paid him a small sum to repair cabinets in the rectory kitchen. Added to his other funds, he had just enough to rent a bed in a hostel for another month. That would suffice. Bread and water were always available to be had. If he had learned anything from the priests who guided him through the cathedrals, it was this. God watched over those who walked the road given to them. The sojourner in his obedience would always have enough. Strangers shared meals with him. Shopkeepers offered him temporary jobs. God and all His children dared him to keep going.

After finishing the cabinets in the rectory, Adeo walked the market streets of Marseille. He liked the smell of the brightly colored spices brought across the sea from Algeria and Morocco. He watched the cloaked women scoop up the powder into bags and bicker in their foreign tongue. The deep, brownish reds looked like someone ground up one of the mountains from his homeland. From there Adeo walked past the stands of the artisans and saw their carvings and canvases and jewelry displayed. They watched him carefully knowing he could afford nothing upon which his eyes lingered. His clothes were clean, and he made it a point to bathe often. And yet, his poverty traveled with him like a companion others could always see.

Eventually he came to a small, nondescript bookshop with a hand-painted sign reading 'La Fable'.

Beside the entrance a large window displayed rare books. One of the books was titled *The Grand Cathedrals of Europe*. Adeo recognized the stylized drawings at once. It was the same volume given to him by The Traveler so long ago.

"Go inside," said The Wind. "You were brought here for a reason."

A bell rang as he entered the shop.

He turned immediately for the display but saw it was blocked by a partition.

"May I help you?" a voice asked.

A beautiful young woman watched Adeo from behind the counter. She had thick, dark hair and almond-shaped eyes turned slightly upward. She was thin and almost as tall as he. She wore a cotton dress down to her calves and black worker's boots. He could not place her origin. In Marseille the French were rarely pure-blooded. They were mixed over thousands of years with travelers from across the sea. It was her lips and her mannerisms, her way of moving her hands and her body, that resembled the French. She looked familiar, like he had already met her in his dreams, like they had been on many adventures together in some other time and place.

"I saw a book in the window," Adeo said. "It reminded me of a book I had when I was a boy. I'd like to see if it's the same one."

"Which book?"

"With the great cathedrals."

She came around the counter.

"What do you know of that book?"

"I know it by heart. I once had a copy of my own."

"A shame you no longer have it. That book is very rare. And very expensive, unfortunately," she said. "My name is Zelie."

"I'm Adeo."

Zelie walked to the window partition and unlocked the backing. She pulled the door open and reached for the book.

"We need to close soon. But you can look. Be careful. The pages are fragile."

Zelie handed the book to Adeo. The feel of the cover transported him back to the tiny dwelling in the middle of the desert, surrounded by towering mountains, crowned by the moon. His mother's voice sang from the cook fire. His baby sister babbled on the floor. Before long, he would hear the pattering of hoofbeats to signal his father's return from work. Adeo fought back tears while turning the pages. The cathedrals looked just as he remembered, only now he had seen most of them with his own eyes.

"Would you like to know the price? I don't even want to say it out loud," Zelie said. "The book is really very rare."

"No," Adeo said. He closed the book and handed it back to her. "But I have a question for you. If I come back another day, will you let me look again? I am willing to work to have time with it."

"Of course."

She returned the book to the display.

"And I have a question for you," she said. "Will you walk me home?"

* * *

They walked the streets of Marseille as if they had known one another their entire lives. After only a few blocks she took his arm. They spoke of ideas and dreams and even fears without any barriers between them. They spoke of their favorite storybooks. They spoke of home and family. They spoke of the language of the moon and the stars and the mountains. She lived an hour's walk from the Vieux Port. The hostel where he stayed was an hour's walk in the opposite direction. He did not tell her, and did not mind the disruption to his day.

The path led them beneath Notre Dame de la Garde.

Sitting atop the church was the bright gold Madonna and child. She watched over the city as both caretaker and warrior, mother and queen. Wayfarers from the sea saw the shimmering reflection before they saw the city. She burned as a torch on the horizon promising love but warning of death for those who brought war to the shores. Adeo had visited the church many times to inspect the craftsmanship of the statue. The statue reminded him of his own mother and the life he was forced to leave behind.

He had overcome much.

In the early days of traveling, he became paralyzed with loneliness. Slowly, the pain turned to strength. Adeo fought to scrub their final cries for help from his memory. After that night, he hid inside La Catedral for three days. Angels visited him. Visions filled his heart and his mind. Time stopped moving in a straight line and came to him as a bowl of water in which he could move his finger and create shapes. He drank from the bowl and at once realized he could live forever. The pool of time was within him. After three days he emerged into the dark of night and returned to the place where his family lay. He kissed their dusty faces. He buried them in a single hole, their bodies laid flat, the baby placed gently between father and mother. The house had been burned. The book of cathedrals was reduced to ashes. Everything was gone. Far away, across the valley, a limping white horse stood in the moonlight. It was the same horse his father was meant to train and the same horse whose injury led to their deaths. Adeo did not blame The Horse. What befell his family was not its fault.

The Horse watched Adeo bury the bodies. By dawn it was gone.

"What's wrong?" Zelie asked as they continued walking. "Your face changed."

"She always reminds me of something I wish to forget."

"Your own mother."

"Yes."

"We could have taken a different path. I didn't mean to upset you."

"I like this way."

"Has she gone on to the next place?"

"Yes."

"I'm sorry. Was she sick?"

"She was killed. Like my father and my sister. All of them, killed over a horse."

* * *

Zelie led him to an estate overlooking the sea.

They passed through an iron gate and into terraced gardens overflowing with fruits and vegetables and flowers. A house of white stone could be seen through a tunnel of trees. The great, wooden front door was open to the evening breeze. A maidservant swept the porch.

"This is your home?" Adeo asked.

"It's where I live, yes. It belongs to my uncle."

"He must be an important man."

"Not in the way you might think," she said. "He's an architect of great buildings around the world. Including cathedrals. That's why I wanted you to come. To meet him."

At the corner of the property Adeo saw a rugged workshop. Firelight filled the windows. Inside someone shouted a type of incantation or prayer. A swell of energy splintered across the property. Adeo felt the pulse in his feet.

"What's he doing in there?" he asked.

"I never know. He's a very private man," she said. "Thank you for walking me home. You probably have a long way to go."

"It's not far," he said.

She nodded, not quite believing him.

"Next time, I'll introduce you to him. My uncle. I think he can help you with your dream. But it's better not to disturb him. His work is complicated. Not like selling books."

Adeo smiled. "Or fixing cabinets."

"Perhaps one day the girl selling books becomes a writer of books, and the boy fixing cabinets becomes a builder of cathedrals."

"Anything is possible," he said.

They looked into one another's eyes without knowing how to say goodbye. She leaned in and kissed his cheek. Zelie turned and walked up the path towards the open door.

On the way home, he took an alternative route that did not pass beneath the golden Madonna. She took a different shape in the night. The absence of light revealed a harsher part of her story—one that ended in blood and suffering—and he did not want the joy he felt in this moment to give way to a desire for vengeance.

* * *

When not with her, he wished to be.

When with her, he wished to be nowhere else.

Adeo's plan had been to stay in Marseille long enough to

capture the details of the cathedral and then move on to another city and another church. Now he questioned whether he should stay in Marseille forever. The dream given to him inside the shelter of the mountain began to dim. Maybe Zelie was a better dream. Some days he thought nothing of cathedrals and filled his time writing her poems. He gathered flowers to bundle for her. He carefully prepared small moments that might light up her eyes.

Adeo left the cathedral earlier and earlier and waited near La Fable for her to flip the sign in the window from open to closed. At the lock of the door she turned with a smile and was caught in his arms. They made a game of it.

"Let's go dancing," she said to him one evening.

"I don't know where."

"I will show you a place."

They traveled through streets he had never walked and came to a door hidden at the end of an alley. On the other side he heard music. She knocked and the man who opened the door recognized her. He let them both inside. Zelie took Adeo's satchel and placed it on a table in the corner then pulled him onto the center of the floor where others spun to the music. He had never danced or heard music like this before.

"We will be a mirror of each other," she said. "Give yourself to me."

She extended her hand wide and he took it. She moved her hips to the rhythm of the band and he did too. She pressed into him and he into her. She kissed him and he kissed back. They danced past midnight. Their skin grew sweaty in the candlelit room. They moved in unison until her movements were his and his were hers and there was no distinction between the two of them.

The hours passed and eventually the barkeep rang a bell signifying that the place would be closing. They did not hear the first time, or the second. They remained pressed wet into one another at the center of the floor.

"You have to go," the man demanded.

Adeo blinked as if out of a trance.

"Come on," Zelie said.

They returned to the table where they had left their things on arrival. Adeo came to a stop. The table was cleared. The satchel, and his notebook, were gone.

* * *

Standing in the garden Zelie wept for his loss.

He refused to allow himself to be discouraged, not after the greatest night of his life. In time he would reflect upon the years of work and prayer and risk required to develop his drawings now in possession of a thief who would have no use for them. But tonight all he saw was her. The sweat upon her neck glistened in the moonlight and he pulled her close. He wanted to be closer still. Closer than nature would allow, closer than anyone had ever been to another human being. He wished to surrender unto her, and for her to surrender unto him. He wished to be integrated fully into her blood, partnered in the elemental workings of both body and soul.

"Zelie," he said. "I have something to tell you. To ask you."

"Yes?"

He took her in his arms.

The ground trembled and he looked to the workshop window filled with fire. But this time, a figure was approaching them. It stopped a distance from where they stood.

"Are you ready?" the voice asked.

"Yes," said Adeo.

"Follow me."

Zelie said nothing as Adeo moved towards the workshop,

drawn away from her and into the strange world of The Architect.

* * *

Adeo watched him from across the fire.

His body was strong and angular and shaped like the buildings he had lifted out of the earth. In his face were lines carved by a thousand voyages. His eyes, locked on Adeo, dug beneath the skin and laid bare all intended to be hidden. He had the visage of someone acquainted with the dark, like he found the line between absolute good and absolute evil and consciously chose which side to stand on every day. In some ways, he looked exactly like Adeo's memories of The Traveler.

Adeo questioned if it was possible for them to be the same man. They both made him feel like the truth of life had been hidden behind a veil, like a divine power was available to those who knew where to look. The smoke rose between them and passed through a hole in the ceiling by which the stars were visible.

"Zelie says you wish to build a cathedral," The Architect said after some time.

"I do."

"Why would you wish so much suffering upon your life?"

"I've dreamed of it since I was a little boy," Adeo answered. "I have sacrificed a great deal for it."

"And yet, a million fools have selfish dreams that should not be pursued."

"This dream was given to me by God. He showed me the path when I did not even know what a cathedral was," Adeo said.

The Architect was amused by the answer.

"Show me your hands," he said.

Adeo turned them over, palms up.

"The men who killed your family. Where are they now?"

Adeo had not told The Architect about his family. Even Zelie knew very little of what happened. Adeo had the distinct feeling that The Architect could see into his past and was reading through the years of his life like a storybook.

"Some died that night. The others, I do not know," Adeo answered.

"And the man who sent them. Where is he?"

Adeo's jaw tightened at the thought of Abu Faras. He imagined him standing in the street, holding Sufiya while looking at The Horse.

"I haven't been home in many years," he said. "I don't know what became of him."

"Do you harbor hatred for him in your heart?"

"Yes," Adeo admitted. "But it is outweighed by sorrow."

The Architect nodded without judgment.

"Tell the fire which way to go." The Architect motioned down to the flames between them. "Wield the flames with your hands."

"I don't understand," Adeo said.

"I want to see if the fire obeys you."

Adeo waved his hands but the flames did not change. The Architect leaned forward so the fire lit his face.

"You speak the language of the moon and the stars and the mountains. I see that in you. That is a great gift. And yet, they don't obey you. You are not ready to master the elements. And thus, you are not ready to build a cathedral," The Architect said. "Go and marry my niece. She loves you. Raise children. Live a happy life. I will make sure you and she always have what you need. But a cathedral can only be built by mastering the language of the universe, wielding the elements around you, and maintaining purity of heart. Of these gifts, you have none."

With a simple movement of his hand, The Architect extinguished the flames.

* * *

Adeo lay awake in the hostel. Strangers slept around him.

He ruminated on his time with The Architect. He had confessed to holding hatred in his heart. The truth surprised him, as he had not thought about Abu Faras in many years. But all along, a seed of vengeance had been growing.

The Architect was seeking obsession and purity.

He asked nothing of Adeo's knowledge or skills.

Adeo longed for his notebook. Inside were hundreds of sketches and notes that may hold the key to unlocking the mystery. Likely the thief kept the satchel and the pouch of coins and tossed the notebook in the garbage. Who would want drawings of cathedrals except for a madman? Who would spend the rare and precious hours of his life inspecting glass and stone, when there was wine to drink and women to enjoy, money to make and money to spend?

The previous night had been wonderful. The language of the moon and the mountains was also present in the dance between him and Zelie. It lived there, too. The tension they felt between their bodies was eternal. The power generated by their desire would give rise to a thousand cathedrals. It would create the greatest works of art ever beheld by human eyes.

Maybe there are different energies in the world, thought Adeo in the darkness. They work together. They know one another. The energy of love is connected to the energy of the mountains and the moon, and so, too, they are intertwined with the energy of war and oceans and storytelling. They are all connected. Maybe the dreamer who masters one energy is more easily able to master the others, but maybe it takes a lifetime to do so, and only then if God allows it.

Adeo stayed awake all night working through such theories. He had nowhere to place them, no record to keep of them.

* * *

The next morning, Adeo wandered the streets of Marseille until he came to the Vieux Port. The fishermen were already out to sea. He arrived far too late in the day to hear their rumblings about the government and the weather. The smell of their cigarettes had long ago dissipated in the cold fog. Across the sea was Africa, but what was the point of dreaming? What benefit did it bring his heart to imagine an impossible future?

"I am lost," Adeo said to The Sea.

"Then keep going," The Sea said back to him. "To stay still is to stay lost."

"You don't go the way I tell you to go. I have no power over you."

"That is because you lack faith," The Sea said. "I will rise to the man of faith who says, 'Rise!'"

Adeo wondered if he was going crazy. Here he was, a young man with his whole life before him, sitting beside the sea in a faraway land and talking to the winds and the waves.

"I lost everything I worked to find."

"You cannot lose what truly belongs to you," said The Sea. "Maybe it will go away from you for a while, but the tide will always bring it home."

Adeo understood. He did not yet believe, but he understood. The sun grew high overhead, and he walked on. He went back to the place where he and Zelie danced. No one answered the door. He tested the handle and found it locked. He walked to the cathedral and saw parishioners exiting mass. Like Moses their faces shone with the glory of being in proximity to the Lord. Faith came easy to some, and with much more difficulty to others. To believe in the unseen was natural for children.

Adeo found that believing in God, in the way priests and parishioners and children believed in God, was increasingly troublesome. He wanted to believe. He wanted God to believe in him, too.

"What can you do by your own strength?" The Sun asked. "Can you make a woman fall in love with you?"

"I don't know. I know very little," said Adeo.

"If God is real, can He not move a notebook more easily than a heart?"

Adeo saw a trash collector's wagon rolling past.

Sitting on top of the pile was his notebook.

* * *

He sat in the cathedral sifting through the pages. They were now twisted and furled from foul-smelling refuse. A faded crimson washed the corner of every page. Somewhere, hidden in the drawings, was the keystone to what The Architect had sought to find in him.

"You've returned."

Adeo looked up and saw the priest who had been so kind to him.

"I am seeking something," Adeo said. "A hidden thing."

"In your pages?"

"Yes."

"What do you wish to find?"

"How to move mountains," Adeo said.

The priest nodded.

"If it were me, I would simply ask the Lord for faith. It is by faith that mountains are moved. Faith as tiny as a mustard seed."

The priest offered a wrapped loaf of day-old bread to Adeo.

"I don't know how to have more faith. What I once believed has now left me," Adeo said.

"That's the case for all of us. It's why you must ask for it to be returned. Like the tide, you will look up and see that what was once lost is now at your feet."

* * *

Adeo found the gates locked. He looked through the bars at the house in the distance. In an upstairs window, Zelie stood facing the morning in a nightgown. She brushed her hair and let the light shine upon her face.

"What are you doing here?" a voice asked.

The Architect emerged from the gardens. Adeo had never seen him during the day. His face was older than he remembered. The Architect glanced back at the house, but Zelie was now gone from the window.

"I came to speak with you," Adeo said.

"You are not ready to build cathedrals," he said sternly. "It is not for men like you to do. You are dealing with a magic you do not understand and cannot safely wield. You will hurt yourself and others."

"Because I lack the faith," Adeo said. "And it is by faith that mountains are moved. The magic is in faith."

The Architect paused.

"What do you know of faith?"

"Very little. But it is this I wish to learn from you."

"What the builders of cathedrals know better than anyone is that stones crumble. Buildings collapse. The real work of eternal value is being done in the hearts of those who lift the hammer. That is where the true cathedral rises. In the heart. If you cannot understand this, you should not be here."

"I understand this," said Adeo.

The Architect watched him carefully for a moment then walked to the workshop. He returned carrying a rudimentary hammer and offered it to Adeo.

"Take this," he said. "Learn how to use it. And pray for faith. Then return in one year."

"I will."

"But before you do, ask yourself if you are willing to die for the calling. Stare into the face of your dream. If it tells you to marry her, marry her. If it tells you to build a cathedral, set her free."

* * *

Adeo waited outside La Fable for Zelie.

The book of cathedrals was gone from the window display. She had replaced it with a book of stories about the great Michelangelo. In some ways he was grateful someone had come along and purchased it. Now he would no longer be teased by the book's presence.

Zelie knocked on the window. He looked up and saw her smiling face. She had been watching him drift away in his thoughts.

"What were you thinking about?" she asked while locking the storefront.

"Nothing," he said. "Old things."

"Are you hungry? I'm hungry," she said.

"Yes."

"Come on. I want to take you somewhere special."

They walked to a restaurant far too expensive for Adeo. She noticed his hesitation but pulled him along nonetheless. The maître de waiting at the front doors welcomed Zelie by name. He bowed as they passed. Adeo often forgot that, unlike him, she had access to fine places. Perhaps her uncle had an account at the restaurant. Perhaps he had accounts at every restaurant in Marseille. They were led to a table in the far corner where bread and wine were already waiting on them.

"You can order anything you'd like," she said. "You don't even have to think about it."

"I have no money, Zelie."

Under the table her hand found his.

"I know. But money is nothing for him, and so it is nothing for me. And so it is nothing for us."

The room was dimly lit by candlelight and by this he looked into her eyes. She was growing more and more beautiful. She had the look of someone who would carry her beauty into old age and even into death. To marry her, as The Architect suggested he should do, would lead to a life of happiness. They could sit at a thousand tables like this one. They could have their own seaside estate. He would hold her in the dawn for a lifetime and together they would raise a family.

"I have something for you," she said.

She reached into her bag and took out a gift wrapped in brown paper.

"What's this?" he asked.

"Just open it," she said.

Adeo thought back to one of his birthdays in the desert, when his mother gifted him a painted rock with an image of the moon. He kept the rock by his bed until the end.

He peeled the paper apart and saw the book of cathedrals.

A storm rumbled within his heart.

The world went quiet. Zelie's shape faded. Her voice disappeared. Her beauty released its hold upon him. He flipped through the pages as if looking into the faces of those who had once dared him into a great adventure and were daring him once more.

"Why would you do this to me?" he asked.

"What?"

He fixed his eyes on the book. He had turned those same pages years ago as a boy while The Traveler sat at the table glancing over at him. Those are cathedrals, he had said. You can find them all over Europe. Adeo had never forgotten those words or the illustrations. They made a home in his heart and never left.

"Adeo," Zelie said. "I thought you'd like it."

"I do. More than you can know."

"Please. Look at me."

He did. She squeezed his hand.

"It's only a gift," she said. "I didn't think it would upset you."

"I thank you for it."

"We don't have to stay here. We can go anywhere in the world. I only want to be with you, wherever it is. Me and you, together."

He said nothing. He turned the pages. The doorway to each cathedral looked like the entrance to El Catedral. The voice called for him to draw near once more.

"Adeo?" she said.

"I love you. I do. And you don't deserve this. But I must go."

Adeo gathered the book and slid it into his satchel. He stood from the table and pushed through the restaurant and into the fading light of day.

* * *

For a year, Adeo did as The Architect instructed.

He learned to use the hammer. The tool and his hand became one and the same. The priest at the cathedral connected him with a guild of tradesmen and they accepted him as an apprentice. The work started early and ended late. They met at a corner of the Vieux Port in the still-dark hours to receive their assignments for the day. Adeo went wherever he was needed. The guild repaired businesses, built new dwellings, and served the church. They scattered throughout the city. Whenever a tradesman was shorthanded, Adeo assisted. He spoke little and worked much.

He avoided La Fable at all costs.

If sent in that direction for a project, he took the long way to make sure he never crossed paths with Zelie. He knew the restaurants and shops she liked best. He knew the pathways lined with flowers where she strolled. He knew the benches where she sat to read and write. In bed, in the tomb of night, he thought of her. He longed for her to be next to him, to feel the warmth of her body. He imagined her in the window with the morning light soft against her skin. Only a fool would leave her.

But with the passing of time, the longing subsided.

Eventually, at the close of the year, he thought of her little, if at all.

* * *

One morning the head of the guild came to Adeo and said, "I hope you are braver than some of these other men."

"What do you mean?" Adeo asked.

"You have a special job today. No one else is willing to do it."

"Whatever it is, I will do it."

He sent him to Notre Dame de la Garde.

Vandals had climbed atop the church in the night and drawn on the golden Madonna with black paint. The act was unthinkable due to the sheer courage it took to face such heights. The church was hosting a wedding that evening and wished to have the defacement removed before more attention was drawn to it.

Adeo was shown through the sanctuary by a priest attempting to withhold his frustration at the inconvenience.

"We have suspects," he said. "Boys. Silly boys with nothing to do but cause trouble. And they will face judgment in this life and the next. I know where they came in, and where they went up. We've addressed it already."

They climbed onto the tower and looked up at the mother

and child gleaming in the morning light. She watched over the sea in glory. The boys had drawn black circles around her eyes and given her a thick mustache curled at the corners. They wrote 'liberté' on her back. Looking up, Adeo now understood why no one else volunteered for the task. To clean her was to risk his life.

"You can use this as a foothold," the priest said. He showed Adeo the path the boys had used to climb the stone and reach the platform. "They survived, somehow."

"I see," he said. "It shouldn't be any trouble."

"Please be careful. The winds will surprise you. There is little to hold on to. Would you like me to stay or go?"

"You can go," Adeo said.

He managed his materials up the side of the stone and sat on the base of the platform upon which the statue was built. He wrapped a harness around her body and fastened it around his own waist, then slowly made his way up. He sank his rag into the solution then slid up her back and reached around to her face. The work was slow and arduous. He gripped her hips and eased around to the front of her body. Her eyes stared at him. She transformed into his mother.

"Do you see her?" The Sun asked.

"I do," Adeo answered.

"Do you understand that no one dies, not even one?"

"I do," he said.

"She is here, like she is everywhere. And you are everywhere, too."

Adeo worked all afternoon. By evening the statue was not only free of black paint but also cleaner than it had been in many years. Soot and salt blown off the sea were removed layer by layer. He worked down to the original gold. As the sun set on the horizon, he climbed back down the tower and set his feet upon solid ground. The bells rang.

He heard a cheer below and looked over the edge of the

church to see a crowd lining the pathway outside the main entrance. The priest had told him there would be a wedding, and he wished to have the mother cleaned before then.

Adeo had done his job. The guild was well represented.

He carried his materials back down the path by which the priest had led him and entered the side of the church quietly. The ceremony was finished, but the bride and groom knelt at the altar with their hands joined together in prayer. Adeo tried to pass through unnoticed, but the can of solution scraped against the wall and broke the silence.

The bride looked up.

It was Zelie.

* * *

At year's end, Adeo told the head of the guild that he was leaving.

Once accepted, men rarely left the guild. The leaders, wise and tempered, protected their laborers and provided all they would need over a lifetime. When seduced by the thought of staying, Adeo recalled the hushed conversations he heard late into the night between his father and mother who lamented that Abu Faras had imprisoned him, even though he was a free man. Adeo feared a commitment to the guild would lead to the same plight that tortured his father.

His father never had a dream beyond caring for those under his roof. He was too simple a man to fill his imagination with faraway lands. He trusted horses, and day wages, and survival. He trusted water in the canteen. He trusted food on the plate. Adeo was not like him. His father, had he still been alive, would have told Adeo that he was a fool twice over. A beautiful girl with an immensely wealthy family loved him, and he had allowed her to marry someone else. And now, a guild that paid him fair wages and respected his dignity had offered him a lifetime of security, and he was turning away from them.

The dream in Adeo's heart had never glowed brighter.

He would be obedient to the calling.

He would build a cathedral in the desert, even if it cost his life.

He prayed for faith morning and night and shaped his craft in the hours between. A year was not enough to reach the mastery of his mentors, or anything close to it, but Adeo's skills were improving in ways that mystified the other guildsmen.

The head of the guild pleaded with Adeo to stay. He warned him of the foolishness of striking out on his own. Adeo told him about his dealings with The Architect, and, for the first time, he confided his dream to build a cathedral in his homeland.

"What's his name?" the guildsman asked. "This architect of yours."

"I don't know. I only know him as The Architect."

Adeo described his appearance, the estate, and the conversations they had together.

"I know every architect in Marseille. I hate to tell you this, Adeo, but whoever you think you are going to meet is not an architect at all. He may be something, but he is not an architect."

Nonetheless, Adeo turned in his apron at the end of the day.

He walked past the basilica and eventually came to the estate of The Architect.

The gate was open. But the estate was nothing like he remembered.

It looked as if a sheen of magic had been peeled away. The gardens once pristine and beautiful were overrun with weeds. The trees had not been pruned in what seemed like decades, though only a year had passed. Rotten fruit lay on the ground.

The trees were overgrown and the house was not visible from the gate. One year earlier he stood in this exact place and saw Zelie in the upstairs window. Where was she now?

Adeo walked through the garden towards the house. He saw no caretakers, no maidservants. On approach he realized the house was completely shuttered. The windows were covered in large boards and the door barred shut with a great wooden beam. Vines grew up the walls.

Adeo thought back to the guildsman's warning.

He knew of no architect fitting the description Adeo gave him.

Adeo rushed down the path and to the workshop. Unlike the house he found the door unlocked. Inside, the room had been emptied out, except for the fire pit in the center of the floor. At the bottom of the pit a single coal still burned orange.

A strong east wind blew hard and fast through the room.

"Are you a man of faith?" a voice asked.

"Yes," said Adeo.

"Show me."

Adeo looked down at the smoldering coal. He held his hand above it.

"Rise up," Adeo said.

The flame stirred and the pit alighted with a roaring blaze.

PART III

The Man and The Magician

Adeo returned home.

The town once small and built on a single street was now unrecognizable. Streets like veins splintered in all directions and gave rise to rows and rows of buildings. Standing in the middle of the Main Street, Adeo felt the same weight on his chest as he did when he was a boy. In those days, he and his father traveled here for supplies, but Adeo always found the desert to be a more civilized place than town. He hated the smell of sewage, the salesmen running alongside their horses, the women trying to lure his father into dark doorways. The old general store was gone. Nothing was in the same place. The world accelerated in his absence towards a future he did not fully understand.

"Move!" a voice cried out.

A horse-drawn carriage sped down the street and narrowly avoided running him over. Adeo tucked away to the side of the street and leaned against a railing to regain his bearings. He felt his pockets to make sure no one had robbed him.

Most of the money he saved working with the guild was spent on passage across the sea. What little he had left over was meant for supplies. He needed a tent, a bedroll, simple tools, and cookware at minimum. He would also buy a new journal. The plans for the cathedral had long been solidified in his mind, but he desired to commune with God through the movement of his pen on the page.

"What are you looking for?" a voice asked.

Adeo turned and saw a woman watching him from the porch. She pulled the hem of the dress up beyond her knee and past her thigh. She smiled. The shape of her eyes reminded him of a snake.

"Supplies," he answered.

"Supplies for what?"

"A camp. In the desert."

"There's nothing in the desert. Nothing for you, nothing for anyone." She moved closer and bent down so her narrow face was near his. She smelled of floral perfume and sulfur. "Out in the desert you will find nothing but death. It will swallow you up and forget your name. I've seen it. Over and over, I've seen it."

"I'm no stranger to the desert," Adeo said. "Or to death."

"The men who go out there, they go crazy and die," the woman said. "Burning under the sun. Choking on sand. Poisoned by snakebites."

"Who sells supplies?" Adeo asked.

She smiled at him.

"It will cost your life."

"Yes. I know," he said. "Now tell me who sells supplies."

* * *

An outfitter drove him to the valley between the mountains. Adeo pointed the way. The mountains watched him carefully but did not recognize his face or his smell. He had been away too long. They remained silent in his mind and in his heart as the wagon wheels rolled over the hard and unforgiving ground. Where once a dwelling stood and a family lived, now there were remnants of wood and ash and nothing more. On the ground, stones still marked where his father, mother, and baby sister were buried.

"Here," Adeo said.

The outfitter pulled the team to a stop.

"Here?" he asked.

"Yes."

"I don't mean to interfere in your business, but this is no place to start over. You aren't going to make it, I'm afraid."

Adeo dismounted the wagon. He and the outfitter pulled the canvas and supplies out of the back. Adeo had purchased enough to survive for the next two months. He had no horse and no way to return to town. He had no access to water.

"I feel like I'm leaving a man to die," the outfitter said.

"I'll find my way back if needed."

"You don't have water."

"There is an old well around here somewhere. I'll dig it out."

The outfitter shrugged his shoulders. "Through that mountain pass, about an hour's ride, is the ranch of a man named Abu Faras. You get sick or snakebit I'd go there first. Closest thing to a town you've got. But he's an unforgiving man. Know that before you cross over. He'll also give you a job, if you're looking for one, and if you know your way around horses."

"I won't need him," Adeo said, now realizing that Abu Faras was indeed still alive. "Thank you."

The man shook his head in dismay. He climbed into the driver's perch and whipped the reins. Soon the horses and wagon were out of sight.

Adeo spent the evening digging out the old well upon

which his family once depended. The water was filled with sand but drinkable if filtered out. In time it would draw up clean. He then dug holes to bury tent posts. Once the moon had risen, he unrolled his bed and lay on his back looking up at the stars.

"I remember you," he said.

"We don't remember you," said The Stars.

"I've been gone for a long time, but I've come home."

"Tell us your name," they said.

"My name is Adeo."

"We have not heard that name in many years. It once belonged to a boy we loved."

"That boy is me," said Adeo.

The Stars went quiet.

* * *

He would build the cathedral on top of the buried bodies of his family.

Like St. Peter's in Rome or Santiago de Compostela in Spain, he would build the church over their tombs. His father was no saint. He lacked interest in spiritual things and knew no prayers by heart. He cursed his luck, from time to time. His craftiest schemes and greatest plans never reached beyond mere survival. He worked with an animalistic commitment to making it from one day to the next. But in doing so he cared deeply for those to whom he was responsible, both horses and men alike. The saints of old had no families. They had no hungry children waiting for them at the end of the day. To die cost nothing because no one would suffer in their absence, so they could risk death on the open seas or in hostile lands or in defiance of kings. They had the terrible luxury of isolation. The family man, on the other hand, had to live more cautiously. To throw himself into the wind was to abandon the only purpose he knew with certainty.

By dawn, Adeo was already working.

He used stones to hold open the pages of his journal. The centermost spread showed an aerial view of the cathedral's dimensions. He measured the lengths of the exterior walls and drew lines in the sand with a shovel.

When Adeo was satisfied that he had measured the footprint of the cathedral with precision, he climbed high up on the mountains and looked down at the shape below.

The tombs of his family were marked in the exact center.

"Tell us what's inside your heart," The Wind said.

"It is a dream. To build a cathedral right down there," Adeo answered. "Will you help me?"

"We don't remember you."

"I am the boy who once wandered this valley in the twilight. My feet have tread upon the stones that have been lying here for a thousand years. My voice sang to the moon. My hands caught the rain. I have eaten of the animals that walk these mountains. Buried in the ground are my father, mother, and sister. I wish to know if you will help me, or if you will watch me die."

But The Wind was gone.

* * *

Every night, he sank into dreams that became indistinguishable from reality.

Often, Zelie walked through the camp in her wedding dress. He sat up and saw her shining like a star beneath the moonlight. Sometimes she spoke invitations for him to come home but usually she said nothing. She watched from across the dying embers of the fire. She observed him and wrote in a notebook. She was becoming more and more beautiful with time. In the mornings he found her footprints all around the camp. The space between the world of dreams and the world of the desert was thin and easily transversed.

"This is what you chose over me," she said one night. "Death in the desert. For whose sake but your own?"

Adeo sat up with difficulty.

His muscles were so sore that he could hardly move. His skin was covered in a thick layer of sand and sweat. The cathedral was little more than scraped lines in the sand and a few holes that had required the entirety of his strength to dig. He could have been waking up next to Zelie. He could have walked her to La Fable in the dawn light and taken her out for dinner at day's end. They could have read poetry to one another in the still of night. She could have been the mother to his children and together they could have made a wonderful and fulfilling life together. Instead, he was here, alone, digging in the sand.

"I didn't have a choice," Adeo said. "I was cursed with a dream. Blame God before you blame me."

But she was gone.

Adeo tried to sleep. She was still nearby. She circled the camp in the darkness. He needed rest. Each time he neared sleep, he heard footsteps. Finally he threw the blankets aside and rose to face her. He meant to run her down. He would grab her by the shoulders and demand she leave him forever.

But standing at the edge of the moon's light was a white horse.

Adeo recognized it at once, the very racehorse his father was tasked with training. Only now The Horse was ragged and desert worn. Its mane was tangled and its coat covered in sticker burs. Various scars marred its aged body. The Horse whinnied at him with whatever power remained in its chest.

"I know you," Adeo said gently.

He tried to remember if his father ever gave The Horse a name. No, his father always said, 'The Horse', and everyone knew which one he meant. The gift was meant for Sufiya and she would have been the one to name it. Adeo walked forward into the night. The Horse hobbled backwards in retreat. The moon and the mountains watched him. The stars did, too. Adeo was barefoot and shirtless. All the heavenly bodies recognized something familiar in him. They smelled him. They listened to the pattern of how his feet landed upon the earth. Perhaps he was indeed the same boy who once tread the valley and cast his great dreams into the skies to be shaped and amplified. Perhaps he was the one sung to sleep by the woman resting deep in the ground.

Adeo followed the white shape through the valley.

The Horse never allowed Adeo to draw close.

"Come to me," he said.

The Horse whinnied in warning.

Right then, a pain ripped into Adeo's ankle.

He looked down to see a red snake slithering away. The poison in his blood stung like fire. He tried to walk but found his foot did not work. He stumbled.

The stars circled until they blurred into a single white light.

Adeo fell and the light swallowed him.

* * *

He awoke in total darkness.

The stinging pain in his leg was gone.

Adeo felt for his surroundings. The floor was made of stone. The air around him was thin and cold, like he was in a cavern. He struggled to sit up.

"Be still," a voice said. "The medicine needs time."

Whoever spoke was no more than a few paces away, but Adeo still could not see him through the dense black.

"Where am I?" Adeo asked.

"You are in a safe place."

"Who are you?"

"I am your friend," the voice said. "Let your body heal."

"What happened to me?"

"You were struck by a snake. A snake whose poison I did not recognize. I believe it was sent here to kill you."

The face of the snake-eyed woman materialized before him and a terror filled his heart.

"I'd like to wake up," Adeo said.

The man placed his hand on top of Adeo's. He was warm. He squeezed gently.

"You are awake, I'm afraid. And it's my job to keep you alive."

Footsteps echoed in the distance. The man was moving away from him.

"Wait!" Adeo called.

Hours passed. He realized that his leg was not healed, but rather it was numb along with the rest of his body. If he tried to move, his body disobeyed him. In the total darkness he had no way of knowing whether it was day or night. He fell in and out of sleep.

"Tell me where I am," Adeo said to The Darkness.

"You are in a good place," The Darkness said back to him.

"I am a prisoner."

"No," said The Darkness. "You are being brought back to life."

When he could no longer bear the silence and stillness, Adeo heard the footsteps returning. With them came flickering firelight. The man appeared holding a torch at the end of a stone corridor and stopped. At first, Adeo thought it was The Architect. But as the man drew closer, Adeo noticed small differences in their faces.

"Stand up and follow me," the man said.

Adeo did. His body obeyed now, but the pain had returned to his leg. He hobbled through the stone corridor. The pathway he walked was not carved by a man, but rather by the hand of God in the ancient days. Adeo was certain he was in the depths of a cave. The light carried by the man faded.

"Don't leave me alone," Adeo said.

"Keep walking. There is only one way."

Adeo felt the wall to his right and used it to guide him forward. Finally, he came to a large opening lit by candles. In the light Adeo looked down to see his leg wrapped heavily in bandages. He shielded his eyes after so long in the darkness.

The man was bent over a table covered in various herbs and glass bottles. The space had bookshelves, work benches, and a bed in the corner.

"What do you remember of the last three days?" the man asked.

"Very little. Other than your kindness to me," Adeo said.

The man nodded.

"Did anyone come to you? In your dreams?"

"Yes. A woman I saw in town."

"Did she resemble a snake?"

"Yes," said Adeo.

The man turned and once more Adeo thought it was The Architect. But something in his face was different. He seemed older and more worn from the desert. The man handed Adeo a cup filled with warm liquid.

"Drink it."

Adeo did so.

"You will live," the man said. "I wasn't sure three days ago, but now I am. God has preserved you for a purpose I do not yet know."

"Where am I?"

"I will show you."

The man led him through a passage of the cavern to a place Adeo recognized from his boyhood. There, on the ground, was where he once sat begging God to let him live, his heart pounding with fear. Through the opening of stone was the vastness of a desert night.

"You are in La Catedral," the man said. "And I suspect you have been here before."

* * *

"Long ago, they called me The Magician. I don't know what they call me now," the man said. "They don't call me anything, I suppose."

They sat across from one another at his table eating bread, honey, and dried meat. The old man told the story of how many years ago he went from town to town performing magic shows. He made objects appear and disappear to the applause of crowds. He put cards and candies in the pockets of people standing far away. He manipulated matter through space and time. In every new place they welcomed his arrival with great anticipation. He performed in streets, in great halls, before governors and barons. Until one day, the story began to spread that The Magician was not simply performing tricks with sleight of hand. Rather, he was harnessing real magic. He was consorting with spirits and tapped into worlds inaccessible by any who had not sold their soul to dark forces. Priests and preachers and moralizers protested his act. Now his arrival was met by raging mobs. They burned his supply wagons. Onlookers stood up in the crowd and shouted that he was a friend of The Devil. They beat him in the streets. With nowhere else to go, he retreated into the desert and made his home in the unforged depths of La Catedral.

"It was true, what they said," The Magician said. "Not that I was a friend of The Devil, but that I was changing reality. Not simply altering their perception of reality, but changing reality itself. Those are two different things. When you begin to understand the universe was built upon a Word, everything is possible. Reality becomes malleable, so long as it is in accordance with the will of God. Nothing exists until it is spoken, which means anything that can be spoken can also be brought into existence."

The Magician covered the half-eaten loaf of bread with a towel, and when he removed it, the bread was a full loaf once more. He tore off a chunk, dipped it into the bowl of honey, and ate.

"I think, now, God wants to show you that there is no end to His abundance," he said, noticing Adeo's hesitance to reach for more bread. "Tell me why a man like you is wandering around the desert in the middle of the night, with no horse and no clothes."

Adeo looked up. The Magician was watching him closely. He seemed to know more about Adeo than Adeo knew about him.

"I think you already know the answer, somehow," Adeo said.

"And how would that be?"

"You've been watching me."

"I have felt a change in the atmosphere. Long before I found you cold and dying on the desert floor. The moon and the stars have been speaking of it, too. Snakes are crawling out of their holes. Ghosts and angels and demons are passing through the veil. The stones are crying out." The Magician pushed the plate of bread towards Adeo. "You've come to build a cathedral."

"Yes."

"And you grew up in these lands."

"Yes."

"And God put a dream in your heart when you were young."

"Yes."

"And you are willing to let it kill you."

"It has already killed me," Adeo said.

The Magician nodded.

"Ours is a land in desperate need of faith," he said after some time. "And you, I think, are a man of faith. Faith in what, is the question."

"I have faith in the dream."

"Yes. But is the dream for your own sake, or for the sake of the world?"

Adeo had not considered the difference.

"I don't know," he admitted. "I have only thought of building what I see in my imagination, and nothing else."

"If you can shape your dream to the benefit of the world, rather than simply the benefit of your own ambition, all forces seen and unseen will come to your aid. Now, eat."

* * *

Adeo waited for the sunrise.

He considered the words The Magician said to him. The cathedrals in Europe always welcomed him as a son. And yet, the builders of those cathedrals did not know him. They never could have imagined the orphan boy who would one day cross the ocean and walk through the doors with a notebook and a dream. But inside of each cathedral, he sensed it was designed for the awakening of his own heart and mind. The vision was not for their own sake, but for the sake of the world.

There was a mystery to the work.

His notebooks said as much.

His heart said the same.

Adeo studied the movements of light. He noted how sound traveled through the space. He obsessed over how one stone melded into another. Some of the mysteries could be explained away by the immense skill of the craftsmen. The rest required a different, more enigmatic explanation. The builders worked in conjunction with the angelic realms. The Creator with all His many faces and all His many children longed for the cathedral to be built even more than the builders longed to build it, and so He guided their hands. The men who poured out their energy became unknowing vessels of a greater power at work in the world.

The sun crested over the distant mountains and filled Adeo's eyes with light.

"Hello, boy. I remember you now," said The Sun. "Have you seen what you need to see?"

"Yes," said Adeo.

He stood with difficulty. The pain in his leg was healing slowly. At night he removed the bandages and applied the paste given to him by The Magician. He was instructed to return to La Catedral when the paste ran out. The Magician said all things seen and unseen would conspire in his favor if only he offered his work to the benefit of the world.

He imagined the people walking the streets of town.

He thought of the children leaping into the sea by the old fort in Marseille.

He thought of the faces he saw on the streets of Europe.

They all needed a place to go, and he would give it to them.

Adeo turned to pull on his boots. There, piled next to the tent, was a heap of stones delivered overnight. He knew not where they came from. There was just enough for a hard day's labor, and no less, and no more.

"I am not ready for you," Adeo said. "I have yet to dig the foundation."

"Then start digging," said The Sun.

* * *

The Horse watched him work.

Day after day, month after month, the creature appeared on the horizon and stood silhouetted against the skyline. Adeo gave up on calling him in. He gave up on offering food or water as bait. The Horse limped in the distance and faded away with the going of the sun. Adeo was not sure if he resented The Horse for the death of his father, or if he pitied him. All the years he was overseas, The Horse was here, surviving alone in the mountains. He had been abandoned to death by no fault of his own. Abu Faras once valued him with a fortune. Now, he was not worth the cost of feed.

Adeo dug the foundation deep into the earth.

Other creatures came to watch the strange man work. Lizards sat on the edge of the well for hours at a time. Coyotes ran through the hole at night. Birds circled overhead. The pile of stones watched, too.

The dream intrigued the universe and so the universe paid attention.

Adeo's beard grew. His muscles strengthened. He became lean and intense and efficient in his movements. He patterned his life with a rigid devotion to the work. His only day of rest came on Sundays, when he slept for as long as his body and mind would allow.

It was on a Sunday when Adeo lay sleeping through the dawn and was awoken by footsteps outside the tent.

He quietly reached for the blade beside his bed, expecting raiders to seize upon him at any moment. Adeo slowly peeled back the flaps of the tent and looked out to see The Horse staring back at him. The healed wound on its once-broken foot was noticeable. The skin bulged and had grown over with matted fur and scars. His mane was long and twisted with thorns and brush. His stained coat was overgrown and missing patches. The Horse hardly resembled the magnificent creature showcased around town by Abu Faras.

"What do you want from me?" Adeo asked.

The Horse jolted at the sound of his voice but did not back away.

Adeo stepped out of the tent.

"Do you know who I am?" Adeo asked.

He approached slowly with his hand outstretched.

* * *

Adeo and The Horse learned to work together.

He fastened a rudimentary strap system to The Horse's back and by this they hauled dirt out of the foundation. The speed of work doubled, even with The Horse's limitations. Together they labored moving the loosened earth from one place to another. The foundation was taking shape. Slowly, the outline of what would one day hold the weight of the cathedral formed in the desert ground.

Often at day's end Adeo climbed the mountains to look down at the progress they had made. The Horse, too tired from the work, did not climb and stayed behind at the camp drinking water drawn up from the well. Sometimes The Horse wandered off and came back days or weeks later. But he always returned.

In the hot midday hours Adeo asked questions about his father and what happened on the day The Horse broke his leg.

The Horse revealed nothing of the past.

Adeo, too, began to speak less and less until he said no words at all. He lived to work and one day die. He became like an animal, pawing up dirt, and, when thirsty, sinking his face into the water.

* * *

A drought through summer and fall both dried the well and shriveled up the small gardens Adeo had nurtured. The Horse left in the night. Adeo supposed the old creature had finally decided to lay down and die. He did not blame The Horse, if so.

He, too, wished to lay down and die. His body lacked the energy to work and with age he was already slower and slower out of bed in the mornings.

He had no money and no food. With the drying of the well, he had no water.

He had nothing but an unfinished hole in the ground.

"This is no way to die," Adeo said to The Moon.

"I have seen many men die like this," The Moon said.

"It wasn't supposed to be this way."

"How was it supposed to be?"

"I wanted to build a cathedral."

"No one builds a cathedral on their own. It takes thousands of men and hundreds of years. It takes infinite wealth and the mighty hand of kings."

"If only I had enough to eat," Adeo said. "I, too, would be a king."

"What kind of king would you be?" The Moon asked.

Adeo thought back to the feast he shared with The Magician. It was the last time he had tasted honey or beef or fresh milk. Many days had passed since he returned from La Catedral. Back then, Adeo was freshly shaven, and his eyes were filled with light for the journey ahead. He owned no mirror but by the touch of his beard and the rough texture of his skin he wondered if The Magician would even recognize him. His hands were misshaped and hardened from ramming the shovel into the ground over and over. His clothes were but tattered rags.

At dawn he left his camp and shuffled across the desert floor to the strange mountain. When he finally arrived, he hit his knees.

"Help," Adeo said into the opening. "I need help."

In time a voice answered, "Why have you stopped speaking?"

"I am speaking now," Adeo said.

"Then come inside," said the voice.

He pulled himself off the ground and slid through the opening of stone. There he collapsed.

* * *

Adeo's eyes came into slow focus.

The Magician stood over him.

"You should have come to me sooner," he said. "As I instructed you to do. Now, you're dying."

Adeo's ribs showed clearly through his skin. His fingernails were discolored. The corners of his eyes were red with blood. Somehow The Magician had not aged, like he was a part of some other realm that did not obey the rules of time and space.

"I inspected your wound. Where the snake bit you. Did you know it's infected?"

Adeo's pant leg had been rolled up. The old scar was inflamed and sensitive to touch.

"No," said Adeo.

"Hold still. This is going to hurt."

The Magician applied a cream to the wound.

"We call it a snake because we have no better word for it in this language. But that was no snake. Do you understand?"

"Yes," said Adeo.

"It was sent here from another place. To keep you from finishing the work to which you have been assigned. The poison is all but impossible to remove."

"I'm hungry," Adeo said with difficulty.

"Yes. Because you haven't eaten. And you haven't eaten because you haven't asked, and you haven't asked because you lack faith."

Adeo pulled his body off the ground and into a nearby chair. The Magician's den was as he remembered. In the center of the room was a table and surrounding it were other stations with vials, potions, and stones for experiments. The walls were lined with books.

The Magician thought for a while then said, "There is a very old story about Jesus the Nazarene. He went into the desert for forty days. While he was there, The Devil came to him and offered to turn stones into bread so that Jesus could eat, but he would only do so if Jesus forfeited his purpose. What would you forfeit today in exchange for bread?"

The Magician filled a cup from a pitcher of water and handed it to Adeo. He drank slowly at first, then emptied the liquid down his throat.

"I have nothing to offer you," Adeo said.

"You could make a promise. That you will eat from my table and then leave this desert forever. Leave your tools. Leave your camp. Leave your hole in the ground. Go find the love of your life and try to enjoy whatever days you have left. Do not waste your precious and fleeting hours on this foolish dream that has haunted you since you were a boy."

The Magician went to the table. He blocked Adeo's view, but when he moved, the table was filled with food. Adeo saw a bowl of grapes in addition to bread and fresh meat.

"You may join me," The Magician said. "And eat your fill."

"At what cost?" Adeo asked. The medicine now stung his leg. The wound bubbled. His stomach ached with intense pain.

"I told you." The Magician plucked a grape from the stem and ate. "Leave this desert forever. Find a new dream."

"Then I choose to die," said Adeo.

"For the sake of the cathedral?"

"Yes."

The Magician sat at the head of the overflowing table. He filled his plate and ate. He poured a chalice of wine and drank.

"How do you think I came to have grapes and wine in the depths of a cave? Have you seen gardens near the entrance?

How might I have fresh milk when there are no cows from which to harvest milk? Have you considered these things?"

"Yes."

"And what is your conclusion?"

"None of it is real. You are presenting an illusion to me."

The Magician tossed a grape to Adeo. He caught it.

"If that grape is not real, then what is real?"

Adeo rolled the small, plump fruit between his fingers but resisted the urge to eat.

"Maybe you are The Devil, like they said," said Adeo.

The Magician laughed aloud. "Far from it. You could even say The Devil and I do not get along so well. Because I know things he wants no man to know. Things he wishes for us to forget."

"Tell me about these things," said Adeo.

"I have already told you, but you did not listen. You are blinded and deafened by your foolish and selfish ambition. The universe was built upon a Word. Matter cannot exist without the preceding Word. The nameless thing cannot exist. If you wield the Word, you will always have what you need. But you keep on ramming your shovel into the ground like a fool."

"Then how do I learn to speak?" Adeo asked.

The Magician smiled. "Now you have finally asked the right question."

* * *

The Magician sent him home three days later with rations and seeds. In the depths of the cave he taught Adeo the Way of The Word. All things depended on one another. Creation was woven with ties from one potential thing to another potential thing. Such was the basis of faith. A potential thing had to believe in the good future of another potential thing. Holding them together and sustaining their purpose through darkest night was The Word. The universe had been designed in this way by God Himself.

The future longed to exist. It only needed someone to come along and name it.

From far off Adeo saw the shape of The Horse against the brightening sky. Only, another horse stood beside it, and between them stood a woman.

He heard her singing as he drew near.

Adeo came to a stop while still a safe distance away. He crouched in the silent dark.

"I see you," the woman said after some time.

"Who are you?" Adeo asked.

She wrapped her arms around The Horse's neck. The sun bled over the horizon and filled her face with light.

"Sufiya," he said quietly.

Her dark hair against the white coat of the horse accentuated her primal beauty. She wore all black and carried a pistol of gold on her hip. The scar on her cheek was still visible and had darkened with time.

"You've found him," she said, running her hands through The Horse's mane.

"He found me."

Adeo walked forward until she was within reach. They said nothing and looked for the child in the other. But both children had died long ago.

"Where have you been?" she asked.

"Far away from here."

"I'm sorry. I never had the chance to say that. For what was taken from you," she said.

He refused to look towards the graves of his family and appear weak to her. She had never known his parents, as he had never known hers. As children they lived in a world of their own, the sole inhabitants in a land of moons and mountains that sang back to the ones who loved them.

"It was a long time ago," he said. "And not your fault."

"I recently heard rumor of a crazy man digging a hole in the desert. I had to come and see for myself. When I saw where, I knew it had to be you. My Adeo. Finally back from the dead."

Sufiya continued running her hands down The Horse's neck. She pressed her forehead against its nose.

"I wanted to bring you with me," Adeo said. "But there was no time."

Sufiya looked up with a smile.

"I have always belonged here," she said.

"I have always belonged here, too."

"Yes. You have," she said. "Which is why I need to ask something of you. It won't make any sense, but you must trust me."

"I do."

"I want you to come with me to a birthday party for my grandfather," Sufiya said.

A fire filled Adeo's eyes at the thought of celebrating the life of Abu Faras.

"Sufiya," Adeo said.

"I know. Please. You don't have to say it. Inside your tent you will find clothes. Fine clothes. Meet me in the mountain pass in one week. At sunset. I will be waiting for you. Everything will make sense in time."

Sufiya drew close to Adeo. He felt her breath on his lips.

"You are still my one true friend," she said. "That has never changed. I will never forsake you, and I will always protect you."

She took his hand and gently placed it upon her scarred cheek.

* * *

He planted seeds in the dry ground. The sky had not offered

rain in many months, but both The Magician and The Architect told him matter was moved and manifested by faith.

"Rise up," Adeo said to the seeds.

Nothing happened. He wondered if he was going crazy. Here he stood in the desert telling seeds to grow out of barren ground.

"What does The Magician know that I do not know?" Adeo asked The Sun.

"Many things."

"I need the rains to come and the seeds to grow."

"And yet, you do not ask. You demand, but you do not ask. What's more, you lack an imagination of faith."

"I don't understand," said Adeo.

"When I look upon the earth, I not only see what is, but what will be. I see the field green when it is still the dead of winter. I see the child grown when he is but a baby. I see the stories in color when the glass is but sand on the desert floor. And that helps me to go on shining."

Adeo stood atop the old well. He looked over the foundation scraped out of the ground. The dirt had not been moved on a Word, but by the sheer strength of his hands and his will.

"I want my dream to come easier," confessed Adeo.

"Is this what you truly desire? To bypass the struggle?"

"Maybe so," he said.

"Did you think a cathedral would be an easy thing to build?"

"I thought God would be more helpful to me. He is the one who gave me the dream. But here I am, dying."

"That is what men do," said The Sun. "They build and die."

Adeo wished to wash the dust out of his throat. He imagined the water deep below him crisp and clean and endless. From the well he could build irrigation systems to the gardens. Out of the gardens he would harvest fruits and vegetables and medicine. In the spring he would gather flowers to place at the entrance of the cathedral. Bees would come and pollinate the buds. Birds and animals would find the paradise and make it their home. He would build fences for cattle and sheep. He would build a proper road to town. Daily, traders would visit the cathedral to exchange flour and tools for stone or anything else he had in abundance. They would enter inside the sanctuary to sing and pray and adore the craftsmanship. His tables would overflow with food and wine. He would feast until his belly was full, and then he would sleep in sheets of silk.

Adeo opened his eyes.

The pile of stones long dormant had yet to be moved.

He had nothing to show for his work but a hole in the ground.

He longed to die and wished God never placed such a foolish dream in his heart.

* * *

Adeo considered killing Abu Faras. The idea tortured him.

Sufiya's invitation provided him a chance that would never come again, to stand face to face with the one who stole the lives of his father, mother, and sister. He imagined the moment. Standing beside her, he could draw a blade and ram it into the old man's heart. This is for my father, he might say.

"Are you a murderer?" The Wind asked him.

"No," Adeo answered.

"Yet you have murder in your heart."

"He must pay for what he did. His curse hangs over the land and keeps the rain at bay."

"Are you the one to collect payment for the sins of men you don't know?"

"His debt is to me."

"His debt is to himself," said The Wind. "Don't you see?"

"Enough. Say no more!"

The Wind stilled.

Adeo stripped his clothes and drew up a small amount of tepid water from the well. He used it to wash his body and shave off his beard. He trimmed the ragged and sweat-matted curls hanging over his ears.

He gripped the blade and saw its sharp edge reflecting sunlight.

He entered the tent and cut through the package she left.

Inside was a suit of crimson red.

* * *

In the mountain pass Adeo saw her outlined against the sky.

Her body was slender and tall. She held the reins of two of her grandfather's racehorses. The wind caught her dark hair and moved it in a dance. He had never come so far in this direction. Always his father told him to go wherever he liked, to make the mountains his home, but the pass was not available to him. Beyond the pass was the kingdom of Abu Faras, and he had no mercy for trespassing boys.

Sufiya watched him from afar as he drew near on the back of The Horse.

"He is still strong," she said as they arrived.

Adeo climbed down.

"He is strong enough," he said.

Sufiya wore a black gown with rugged gold jewelry on her hands, ears, and around her neck. Adeo presented himself in the clothing she gave to him. The package she left included polished boots, a timepiece, and a square of black, silken fabric that matched her dress.

"There is the Adeo I remember," she said, and touched his face now smooth. She folded the square of fabric and tucked it into his jacket pocket. He hoped she did not feel the knife hidden on his hip.

"What would the boy and the girl from long ago say if they could see us now?" Sufiya asked.

"I think they would laugh at us wearing these clothes."

"I think so," she said with a smile. "Tonight, you must trust me completely."

"Tell me what this is," Adeo said.

"A party. Wine and food. Music and dancing. My father's men, their wives, their girlfriends. Officials from town. Bankers. Amongst them will be the men who once abducted me. The ones who did this to my face. They have since made peace with my grandfather. Together they are finalizing a new business deal. All will come one by one and grovel at his feet for favors. And behind his back, they will whisper and scheme for the power that will be left behind at his death."

"They will know I don't belong."

She straightened his collar and lapels.

"That's what the suit is for," she said. "Tie up The Horse or set him free. We have a long way to go."

Adeo set The Horse free.

They mounted the ones she brought. Sufiya turned west and kicked into a dead sprint. He followed her lead. She cut through the desert as a star cut through the night sky. The ground lifted her. With every step the earth made way. She was the queen of the desert and all bowed as she passed. Throughout all the years he had been wandering the streets of Europe, she was walking beneath the same stars and convening with the same mountains. They trusted her heart and came to her aid when called upon.

Atop a distant ridge Sufiya pulled to a hard stop to wait on Adeo. Dust rose around her in the fading light. He arrived and saw the estate of Abu Faras sprawled below. The kingdom was far greater than he had ever imagined. Stables and fields of green stretched in all directions. At the center of the property was a massive house and a courtyard lined with electric lights and filled with guests. From the ridge they could hear the faintest sound of music.

"It will happen fast," Sufiya said. "All of it."

"What do you mean?"

She did not answer but whipped the reins. Her hair and the wings of her dress swirled around her as she descended the face of the mountain like an angel of death.

* * *

They rode slowly past armed guards and through a tunnel of trees lined with lamps. The guards lowered their heads in respect as Sufiya and the stranger passed. They had all been told she would be arriving with a powerful man new to the area who wished to build relationships with other men of means. They came to a large barn where two servants approached them and took the reins of the horses.

"Ms. Sufiya," said one. "Welcome home. Everything is prepared for you."

Sufiya took Adeo's hand and gripped it with all her might as the servants led the horses around the barn.

"Do not look away from him," she said. "Stay with me. We are soon to be married, remember."

"You never said that."

"I am saying it now."

They walked down a pathway of stone towards the sound of music and laughing voices. A servant at the entrance offered them wine on a tray.

"Ms. Sufiya," she said.

"How's the wine?" Sufiya asked.

"Everything is prepared," the servant answered.

Sufiya took no glass and continued walking. Adeo stayed in pace with her.

They entered the courtyard. A band played from a stage

while the guests danced. Others were scattered at tables drinking and talking. On the far end of the courtyard an old man sat in a chair elevated on a platform. He slumped in the chair and watched the guests drink his liquor and eat his food. Tonight he would showcase a brand-new racehorse bought in partnership with the rival family that had once kidnapped a little girl and slashed her face with a razorblade. They sat at the table nearest him.

"When he calls us over, walk like all the world belongs to you," Sufiya said quietly to Adeo. "He's already watching us."

Adeo stood straight. He understood. She wished for him to present himself as a man worthy of marrying the prized granddaughter of Abu Faras.

"Kiss me," she said.

"Now?"

"Yes. As if I am yours."

Adeo turned her by the waist and kissed her lips. She took a deep breath and smiled.

"Very good."

Abu Faras stood up. He was taller and more broadly built than Adeo remembered. Abu Faras motioned across the courtyard for Sufiya and Adeo to come to him. She nodded in submission. She led Adeo through the crowd of people who parted as she approached. In her presence she carried a force felt by all in attendance. Heads turned to see the woman in black, scarred and beautiful and dangerous and lovely all at once. She came to the feet of Abu Faras.

Adeo felt the weight of the blade on his hip.

"You're late," Abu Faras said to her. His voice was weak and fading. "Where have you been?"

She knelt before him.

"In the mountains," she said.

"The mountains," he mocked. "And what did they tell you today?"

"They said that today you will die."

At once, Sufiya reached beneath her skirt and removed the gold pistol. She pressed the barrel against her grandfather's belly and pulled the trigger.

Blood splattered on Adeo's crimson suit as all the world stopped spinning.

Abu Faras fell out of the chair groveling for breath. The old man fumbled his hands over his stomach to stop the flood of blood now dripping off the platform. At the sound of the gunshot most of the guests ran to the exits though some hid behind tables. Other gunshots filled the courtyard as those loyal to Abu Faras were executed where they stood.

Sufiya held the gold pistol at her side. She stood between her dying grandfather and the family who abducted her. Her own guards now surrounded them with guns drawn.

"Do you see me?" she asked the table of men. She cleared the hair from her face to show the scar they had inflicted upon her. The blood of Abu Faras speckled her face. Her eyes burned like coals.

No one spoke. She turned back to her grandfather.

"And you, do you see me?"

He said nothing as the life slowly poured out of him.

She turned to Adeo. "And you, do you see me?"

"I see you," he said.

She smiled and there he saw the little girl who once leapt from boulder to boulder in the recesses of the mountains. A tear ran through the blood speckled on her face. She turned back to the table of men.

"Did you hear that? I will go on being seen. But tonight, you will disappear."

At a casual flick of her hand, her guards executed the family. She stepped over her grandfather's convulsing body and sat in his chair. She tapped her nails on the arms of the chair and stared at him until the light left his eyes.

"Go now," she said to Adeo. "Be free. Build your cathedral."

* * *

The downpour of rain began as he crossed the ridge.

Adeo could not see the path forward and hoped the horse remembered the way. Lightning splintered across the sky and the horse threw him off. He tumbled on the ground as the horse escaped back in the direction from which they came. Adeo's fingers dug into the ground now turned to mud. He crawled forward in search of rocks to find shelter.

On hands and knees he fell into a sudden stream.

He gripped what he believed to be stone until lightning struck once more and revealed he was lying in a riverbed of pure gold.

PART IV

The Old Man and The Angel

Adeo held the stone suspended between earth and sky. He drifted it slowly into place, so the edge of one stone was perfectly aligned with the edge of another.

"There," he said.

"It is a good place," said The Stone, and there it lay.

Adeo collapsed to one knee to catch his breath. Every stone lifted drew from the balance of his remaining days. To build the cathedral was to die. He knew this, as he had always known.

The dream demanded death as payment.

From atop the scaffolding, Adeo looked over the desert world far below. The unforgiving land had been ordered by the work of his own hand. Gardens grew with fruits, vegetables, and flowers. The well once dry provided fresh water not only to sustain Adeo and the gardens, but for the herds of sheep and cattle and horses fenced into pastures. The entrance to the cathedral opened to a courtyard of stone. An unfinished road pointed in the direction of the town. All he had dreamed in his days of despair came true by the grace of God, though not without exacting a tremendous cost from both body and mind. The universe came alongside him to dig trenches and multiply his efforts, but only if Adeo exerted the totality of his strength in doing so. The divine met him at the end of his abilities and not before. But there, in his lacking, a cathedral arose from the desert, and a place of plenty was born from lifeless ground.

He counted three stones left on the ground. Tomorrow, he would awake to find the pile replenished with hundreds more, the daily manna. To place them all meant he had given himself fully to the work.

"How much longer until I am free?" Adeo asked.

The Wind dormant said nothing.

The Sun bright said nothing.

The Moon hidden said nothing.

The Stars unseen said nothing.

The Desert endless said nothing.

"You are free now," said God.

Adeo stood to his feet. By faith he extended his hand. The stone far below rose through the sky and towards the place he directed it.

* * *

He slept on the floor of the sanctuary.

The pews had yet to be built so he laid his mat in the center of the room and looked up through the unfinished ceiling at the stars above. Directly beneath him his parents and sister were buried in the crypt. Alongside them was the horde of gold recovered the night he escaped the home of Abu Faras. He knew not its worth, only that he had taken many trips over the years to transfer it from beneath the sand to the cathedral. He would one day shape the jagged pieces into the form of a mother and child to serve as a crown on the cathedral. She would watch over the desert with a loving and merciful eye while keeping the child safe in her arms.

After the night he came upon the gold, Adeo traveled to La Catedral to seek the counsel of The Magician.

He called into the caverns. No voice answered. He stepped through the opening and walked the corridors with a torch until he was lost deep inside the mountain. He finally came to the place where The Magician showed him the table overflowing with food. Only, The Magician was gone, as were all his belongings. Adeo wondered if he had imagined their interactions, if it was all a fever dream born from the poison of the snake bite.

Until, he found a single grape in the center of the stone floor.

Adeo picked it up.

"Have you learned how to speak?" a voice asked him.

"I have learned that all things are possible with God," Adeo said. "Tonight, I found a river of gold."

"If you found a river of gold in the middle of the desert, imagine all the treasures you haven't found," said the voice. "The world is filled with treasures only to be discovered by those who are able to see them."

He ate the grape. The sweetness filled his mouth. He spent the next days trying to escape the mountain. His torch burned out and left him blind in the darkness. He had only his hands to feel his way down the corridors. At times the voice guided him and at times the voice fell silent.

Finally, Adeo returned to the entrance of La Catedral and there he collapsed in gratitude at the sight of moonlight pouring through the opening.

By then, he knew how to speak, because he knew how to listen.

* * *

Adeo walked the gardens at sunset to pluck ripened fruits from the vine. He gathered them in baskets and set them aside to be traded with the few men who knew of the cathedral and its location. Some came from the town, and others came from the gatherings of tribesmen who still called the desert home. He asked no questions of them, and they asked no questions of him.

Adeo wore a flowing robe of brown cotton. His beard had grown long and wild and gray in the quiet decades, and yet no raiders or thieves came upon the old man. No one disturbed his work. Those who wished him harm were warded off by beings from unseen realms. Figures with eyes of cinder and flame stood afar and watched them travel through the valley. By this they knew not to speak to others of what they had seen, for they believed the cathedral to be cursed.

Adeo loaded the figs into a basket that would be picked up in a day's time. He ate a few from the top. Like all days, the morning began with a pile of stones and ended with the stones placed atop the cathedral. Tomorrow would come and go the same. The following days and years would come and go the same. All of life became an act of repetition.

"She is coming to you," said The Sky.

Adeo covered the basket of figs with a cloth and stood up.

He walked around the cathedral and looked west to see a dozen soldiers led by Sufiya at their head. In their midst was a prisoner blindfolded and in chains. She rode as she always did, with her head angled low and her cheek flat against the horse's neck. The midnight tail of her dress fluttered behind her. When close to Adeo she pulled to a hard stop and sat up straight in the saddle. She repositioned her brimmed hat upon her head. She turned broadside and looked at him with her eyes dark and growing darker.

"You haven't come to see me lately," Sufiya said.

Adeo motioned at the nearly completed cathedral.

"I've been busy," he said.

"So you have."

She smiled and dismounted. The cathedral rose above her. The structure was perfectly symmetrical with a tower at its head. At the center, between four spires, was a platform where soon he would place a golden statue of the mother and child. The front steps led to a series of arched doorways and behind the final one was the sanctuary. At the far end of the sanctuary a staircase led down to the crypt beneath the altar. There he had stored the gold and other treasures offered by the mountains. The windows had all been carved but the stained glass had yet to be created or placed. With the sand at his feet Adeo had all he needed to form the windows. Yet, his work was guided by what was given to him each morning. As long as he awoke to a pile of stones, he would place stones. If he awoke to a pile of lumber, he would build pews. When he awoke to a pile of sand, he would make the glass.

"How long until you're finished?" Sufiya asked. She took his arm as they walked the perimeter of the cathedral.

"The exterior is close. But a lifetime of work remains in the details and ornaments. The statues and the stories."

"No one else in the world could do as you have done," Sufiya said. "Are you well?"

"I am well enough," he answered.

"I worry about you. Sometimes you come to me in my dreams asking for help. But I know it isn't really you."

Sufiya's men stayed mounted. They watched her carefully.

"What has he done?" Adeo asked.

Sufiya looked back at the blindfolded prisoner.

"Show me the inside," she said.

He led her into the sanctuary. Spread upon the altar were blueprints and scattered tools and journals and old books. She moved one aside and found the book of cathedrals given to him by Zelie.

"This one. I remember this one," she said. "From when we were children."

She looked through the pages of the book and smiled. At once Sufiya looked like the girl he remembered, the one who held the darkness at bay, though now her hair was graying and her eyes wrinkled at their edges.

"This is a different copy. That one was lost to the fire," Adeo said.

"But God gave you a new one."

"Yes," he said.

She handed the book back to him. A small red bird flew from corner to corner of the ceiling. It landed upon a carved stone angel with its wings spread wide.

"Men do not deserve such a gift," Sufiya said, in awe of all he had done. "The man in chains. The one you saw. He is unworthy to see this cathedral. He is a thief. He is nothing. I would rather gouge out his eyes than let him see what you have created. The sun, yes. The mountains, yes. You and I, the boy and the girl who have always called this desert home, yes. We belong here. Our hearts are woven into this place. But men like him will come from afar and destroy your dream for no reason at all. They will diminish the beauty just by looking upon it. They will spit on the stones because they need someplace to spit. They will tear the face off what is good just to see if they can."

"And what choice do I have but to offer it to them?"

Sufiya took Adeo in her arms.

"Finish it," she said. "But let it be for us alone. Not for them."

"And when death comes to us, what will become of the cathedral then?"

She kissed his cheek.

"When death comes for us, we'll go some other place. A

wonderful place. And you can dream all over again," Sufiya said. "Until then, I will do what's necessary to protect you."

She turned and walked out of the sanctuary and into the fading light of day. He watched her through the open doorway. She put her hat back atop her head and tightened the string beneath her chin. She pulled on black leather gloves. She looked at Adeo standing in the unfinished shell of the cathedral.

"I will certainly have him killed. The thief," she said. "Not all men deserve to see what you have done. They don't deserve to see the hand of God at work."

She stepped out of his sight.

That night, Adeo awoke to the sound of a gunshot echoing across the desert. He sat up in the dark sanctuary. The red bird fluttered back and forth above, going from corner to corner.

"Go now," Adeo said. "I'm not holding you here."

* * *

The first to arrive was a boy.

Adeo awoke in the gray light of the sanctuary. He tied on his boots and readied himself for the daily work. When he opened the great wooden door to the outside world, he saw a boy no older than ten curled upon the steps unconscious. The boy was covered in dust as if birthed from the womb of the desert.

"He was wandering across the earth and I led him here," said The Desert.

"Where is his home?"

"He is from a faraway place."

Adeo bent down and felt for a pulse. The boy was alive but not responding.

No pile of stones had been left overnight which led him to believe caring for the boy was the daily task before him. Adeo carried the boy to his horse and mounted and rode for town.

There he arrived as a stranger to the modern world of men.

He loathed what the city had become. He detested the smell of trash and smoke lingering in every alley he passed. He hated that men lived with less dignity than animals. And yet, these were the men and women and children who would one day walk through the doors of the cathedral and feel their hearts awakened by what he had created. His dream was meant to be an offering to them.

With the boy draped across the saddle Adeo asked the location of a doctor and was pointed to a building down the street. He tied up the horse and carried the boy into the rudimentary clinic. The doctor sat at a desk reading a newspaper and eating lunch.

"He needs help," said Adeo.

The thin-framed doctor wiped his hands while putting the newspaper away. He affixed glasses over his eyes and squinted at the limp boy.

"What happened to him?"

"I don't know. I found him on my steps this morning. He's breathing but unconscious."

The doctor looked carefully at the boy's face.

"Lay him down over there."

Adeo placed the boy on a narrow bed and rested his head on a pillow.

"Are you his father?" the doctor asked.

"I don't know him."

"Where do you live?"

"Far from here. In the desert."

"Where in the desert?"

"North. Over the mountains."

"North over the mountains," the doctor repeated. He placed a stethoscope over the boy's heart and listened for a heartbeat. "I guess you've seen that church, then. The one they call the cathedral."

Adeo said nothing.

"I haven't seen it myself or met anyone who has," the doctor continued. "But if you live up that way, you must know what I'm talking about. It rose over the top of the mountains a few weeks back. People are asking questions." He removed the stethoscope. "He's breathing. No fever. No wounds. You said he just showed up?"

"He did."

"And there was no blood?"

"He looked like he was sleeping."

Adeo fished in his pocket and removed a shaving of gold. He offered it to the doctor as payment for his services.

"I trust you will care well for him and find his parents," Adeo said.

The doctor eyed the gold shimmering in the dim light. When he looked back up, Adeo was already gone.

* * *

Upon his return Adeo found the door to the sanctuary wide open. He entered the cathedral to see a small campfire lit on the center of the altar. A figure sat on the other side of the fire but was shrouded from view. The figure turned a spittle on which a red snake had been woven and was now roasting to a crisp.

"I killed the snake that bit you," a voice said to him. "All these years it slithered the desert waiting for a chance to strike you again. I found it here, on the altar, and here I crushed its head beneath my heel."

Adeo widened his approach along the far wall.

"Who are you?" he asked.

"A friend," the voice answered. "One who has been watching you for a long time."

Adeo now saw beyond the fire.

It was the boy, alive and alert.

"You cared well for me today," the boy said. "Come and sit. You have traveled far."

Adeo approached the fire cautiously and sat across from the boy.

"My name is Rafa," the boy said.

"Who sent you to me?"

"One who has great interest in the completion of your work."

"You came to test my heart," guessed Adeo.

Rafa picked a chunk of meat from the snake and ate.

"No," said Rafa. "Your heart is known. I came to open the door to the world."

* * *

All night Rafa walked the cathedral and surrounding grounds to inspect the work. The stones held stories and to them he asked what had taken place. They told him of Sufiya and the patricide of Abu Faras. They told him of The Magician. They told him of sicknesses and years of drought and the raiders who had descended upon the cathedral only to be turned away by armies of angels while Adeo slept. They told him of winged figures with eyes of fire and coal. They told him of the young boy who many years ago saw his family murdered and took refuge in the mountain called La Catedral.

"There are no stories on the walls," Rafa said as Adeo tried to sleep. "No statues. No glass. No inscriptions."

"I will add them when the time comes," Adeo said quietly.

"The time has come."

Rafa descended the steps into the crypt.

The wind picked up overnight and blew so hard that in the morning Adeo had trouble standing on the ground. He forced the cathedral door closed. The gates swung off their hinges.

Many of the animals roamed free. The scaffolding swayed back and forth. Adeo pulled the hood of his cloak over his face to protect himself from the sand blowing like tiny darts and looked up to see Rafa standing in the open tower undisturbed as if the wind passed through him.

No pile of stones had been given overnight, nor had any lumber or brick.

"What am I to do?" Adeo asked.

"Tell your story," Rafa said. "In the glass."

The wind swirled upwards before Adeo. He scooped sand into his hands and threw it into the cyclone. He saw Zelie silhouetted against the sea, standing at the Vieux Port on a summer morning. He saw The Traveler blowing breath like steam into the cold dawn as he rode away. He saw Sufiya digging through the sudden stream for gold. He saw The Horse. He saw The Magician carrying his torch through the hallways of the mountain. He saw his mother standing over the cook fire with his sister on her hip. He saw Abu Faras dead. He saw a boy named Adeo talking to the moon and smiling at the wonder beheld. He saw his heart spread upon an altar and a cathedral revealed beneath the flesh.

He saw many things.

The storm blew the sand in his face and he ducked to protect himself. The force of wind became so great that it lifted Adeo's body off the ground and held him suspended. The hand of God played with him as a small child might pluck petals off a flower, then dropped him to the ground. When the winds finally died down enough to look up, he saw panes of stained glass stacked where once the stones lay.

* * *

The next to arrive was the doctor.

He appeared on horseback at midday and rode into the

center of the courtyard. The great cathedral stood before him. Birds circled the tower above and then flew east at the sight of him. The doctor had never seen anything like it with his own eyes. The building looked like some ancient and monstrous worshiper stilled by a spell.

"Hello?" he called out.

The doctor climbed the steps and banged on the great wooden door.

Adeo answered. Behind him Rafa sang into the emptiness of the candlelit sanctuary.

"I knew it was you," the doctor said upon seeing Adeo. "The builder."

"How have you come here?" Adeo asked.

"The same way that many will come," the doctor said. "They are all coming. They all need to see what I see."

His prediction proved true.

In the coming days more and more men and women appeared on the horizon. Adeo and Rafa watched them arrive from the tower. A line of people trod the path from the town to the mysterious cathedral in the desert. Wagons and carriages followed. The pilgrims intended to stay for days, if not weeks. Eventually the grounds were dotted with temporary shelters and tents. Each morning the pilgrims gathered outside the door asking to be let inside, and each day Adeo told them to wait until it was finished.

At first, they sang songs of praise to God.

They joyed in the shadow of the cathedral's magnificence.

They awed at the craftsmanship.

They shared food.

They cared for one another.

They prayed.

They welcomed all who arrived.

They reveled at the sound of work being done inside.

They adored the stories told in the glass.

Until, they grew weary of waiting.

They banged on the door at all hours.

They demanded to know when it would be finished.

They jeered the man inside who dared not show his face.

They called him a devil.

They accused him of wielding black magic.

They fought.

They ate freely from Adeo's gardens.

They gorged themselves until the vines were empty.

They left trash on the steps to be carried away by the wind.

They dug latrines and filled them and dug more.

They contracted and spread diseases.

They claimed ownership over the water well and charged for its use.

They carved out property lines in the sand.

They assembled into groups and angled for power.

They robbed and abused one another.

They committed murder.

They slaughtered Adeo's livestock.

They charged the poor to set up tents.

They depleted all the grounds had to offer.

They snuck off into tents in search of paid pleasure.

They drank themselves into mindlessness.

They rotted with thirst and hunger.

They blamed Adeo for all they came to lack.

They cursed both Adeo and the God who made him.

They began to hate the cathedral and all it represented.

They despised its beauty.

They mocked all that was good and made irony of truth.

They wished to tear the cathedral apart with their bare hands.

They wished they had never come to see it.

They wished it had never been built at all.

* * *

Adeo still needed time.

The Lord provided him marble and bronze to adorn the interior of the sanctuary. The gold statue of the mother would come last. He longed to go slow and to pray, to listen to the marble and hear what shape it desired to become. But the crowds locked out of the sanctuary pressed against the windows. They threatened to break them. He protected the windows with sheets of wood. They climbed higher to look through other windows.

As Adeo stacked the barriers higher and higher one evening, he looked out and met the eyes of the doctor. In the chaos, the frail man sat against the base of a leafless tree watching the rise of the cathedral. Unlike the others, his face shone with peace. Since climbing the steps and knocking on the doors, he had been enthralled by the questions awoken in his heart. The answers were difficult to find but worthy of pursuit. He prayed. He sang amidst the madness. He offered his heart upon an unseen altar and hoped to be transformed into something new. He gently lifted his hand and waved at Adeo. Adeo returned the simple gesture of greeting. Then, he placed the barrier up to block the entirety of the window.

"Not all men are the same," said Rafa. "Some are pure of heart. They wish to be connected to the divine, even if they don't know how to say so."

"They must wait. I need time."

"It is not a question of time. The cathedral belongs to them today as it will belong to them tomorrow. It has always belonged to them. This house of stone is to be their only inheritance. A pathway to eternity. When will you give it away?"

"I will give it away when it's done," said Adeo.

Adeo stopped working during the daylight hours. He became a nocturnal creature. He wrapped padding and cloth around his head to quiet the incessant noise coming from outside. Beyond the windows he heard screams and gunshots and raging voices. They infiltrated his imagination. His work suffered. He no longer labored out of obedience and love but out of haste and angst.

"Tell them to be quiet," he said to The Desert.

"They do not know the language I speak," said The Desert. "They are deaf and blind. Why don't you go and speak to them in the language of men?"

"Because I wish to not think of them at all," said Adeo. "I wish to pretend they don't exist."

Slowly and nonetheless, the alcoves filled with majestic figures and carvings of angels and saints and men of great character.

* * *

One evening, Adeo awoke to complete silence. Gray light filled the sanctuary. He lit the candles at the altar and dressed in his robe to prepare for the night's work.

"Rafa?" he called.

He found himself alone. Every other evening at this time, the crowds outside the sanctuary roared with drunken laughter and rage. They tried to tear the stones apart. They threw rocks at the cathedral doors or tried to climb the tower. Many had fallen to their deaths doing so. He walked down the aisle towards the front door and there lifted the heavy beam that kept the outside world from coming in.

He wondered, for a moment, if everyone had finally listened to his pleas and gone home to give him time.

Adeo swung the door open into a haze of red.

Fire and smoke filled the sky.

Standing before him was Sufiya on a black horse. She held a sword smeared in blood at her side. Tents burned behind her.

The perimeter of the earth was scraped in flame. She peeled the fabric from her face and there looked like an angel of death turned loose upon the godless of the earth.

"My Adeo," she said gently. "Forgive me. I should have come sooner."

Adeo stepped forward into a puddle of blood. His bare foot dripped in crimson. In the darkening evening he could still see the bodies strewn on the ground. They had all been slaughtered. The sand greedily drank up their blood. The slain lay on the ground in shapes he did not immediately recognize due to the brutality by which they had died. Sufiya's warriors rode slowly through the camp and extracted the life from any who were still breathing.

"My men will drag them away," said Sufiya. "And you can finish what you started."

The doctor lay dead at the foot of the stairs, at the same place Adeo once found Rafa. The frail man's eyes were open, though the narrow glasses he wore had been smashed. Adeo rushed down the steps and took up the doctor in his arms. A final breath of air escaped his lungs.

"I warned you," Sufiya said. "They don't deserve the beauty you offered them. I cannot bear to see them make a mockery of what is good. A mockery of all the mystery left in the heart of man. The desert sees you. The stars and the moon see you. I see you. But man is blind."

"I see death," Adeo said. "Nothing more."

"A few more days, and they would have killed you. And then they would have torn your work apart. For no reason. Because their nature compels them towards destruction."

"This is not the way. This was not the dream He put in my heart."

Sufiya dismounted. She met him at the bottom of the steps. Close now he looked for the little girl with whom he had wandered the mountains and sang silly songs to the stars. She smelled the same. Even with the blood and sweat on her, she was inseparable from the nature of the place that raised her. But a darkness had consumed her heart.

"My Adeo," she said. "Beauty depends on death. You cannot have one without the other. You are the carrier of beauty and I the carrier of death. We are one force moving. One force eternal. And the cathedral is ours."

* * *

That night Adeo rode to La Catedral.

He wished to sit at the base of the mountain as he had done as a boy and feel the fear and wonder of looking into the entrance. Back then, his heart was pure. Simple questions captured his imagination and colored his dreams. He filled the gaps of his knowledge with extravagant stories and held them true. Every corner of the desert revealed a new mystery to be explored. The days had no number or end.

He loved life.

He loved the friends that surrounded him.

He loved La Catedral.

He loved its shape, its name, its voice.

Adeo saw the strange mountain looming. He dismounted from a distance and approached on foot. He came slowly to the dark doorway. A bright moon hung over the pointed spire of the mountain. At the entrance he removed his robe and fell to his knees. He slid his hand into the opening and then withdrew it into the moonlight.

"I am the boy who came to you long ago for shelter," Adeo said. "In my darkest hour, you protected me. You held me for three days and gave me new life."

"I remember," La Catedral said. "What do you want from me now?"

"New life, once more," he said. "I am soon to die but need more time."

"What good is it to give an old man more time?" La Catedral asked. "You have lived long enough."

"I fear that I brought death to the world," said Adeo. "And nothing more. I need time to make amends."

"Are you so great a man that with a few more years you can make amends for death?" La Catedral asked.

"I could try," said Adeo.

"You have already tried. By stacking up stones in a place where no one saw them."

"I gave myself to the dream God placed in my heart. What else was I to do?" Adeo asked.

"You are still blind, old man. You see what you see, but not what God sees."

The moon went dark. He grew angry that La Catedral was mocking him.

"You are a cursed mountain," Adeo said. "You mock those who come to you in good faith."

"I have spoken to the stones," said La Catedral. "The ones you have been stacking on top of one another. In the quiet of the night, they whisper across the desert to tell me of the work being done. You say that you are using them to build a cathedral. And yet, they say they are building a cathedral in you. Which of these stories is true?"

"I don't know the truth anymore," Adeo said. "Maybe I have never known the truth."

"Did you know the words the poet writes are also writing poetry in him?" La Catedral asked. "Did you know the one who explores the great beyond is also being explored by the great beyond? The thing you are building is building you. Old man, you were not made to build a cathedral, but to become one. To understand this mystery is to die. To understand this mystery is to be born again. Only then will your heart be restored to you.

Only then will you be ready to make of yourself an offering to the world."

Adeo said nothing.

He sat before the opening until night's end and prayed for eyes to see.

* * *

In the dawn light he saw the grounds had been cleared of the dead.

Far away, towers of smoke rose into the sky. He smelled burning flesh on the wind. The fences were torn down. All the livestock had been eaten or prodded to death for sport. The gardens once generous had shriveled into cracked roots. Adeo tried to draw up the pail of water from the well but found the rope had been cut. The bucket lay deep in the earth in diseased water.

"If it all led to this, then what was it for?" a voice asked.

Adeo turned to see Rafa standing atop the landing where he planned to place the statue of the mother and child.

"I wish to be free of this burden," Adeo said.

"You can never be free of the thing you were born to become."

Adeo picked up shredded tent fabric stained with blood.

"I wanted them to see and remember. To walk through the doors and believe they are more than flesh and blood. I wanted the voice of God to echo through their chests. That they might see beyond the illusion and remember that we are eternal."

"Have such men as these the capacity for remembrance?"

Adeo looked across the wasteland once lovely.

"That is for God to know," he said. "My purpose is to build the cathedral, not to save the world."

Adeo walked into the cathedral and descended the steps to the crypt. He lit a candle to bring light into the cavern. There

Rafa was already waiting for him. For all that had been plundered and destroyed, the horde of gold was safely stored. Adeo understood the cathedral was to be finished that night. Any great kings of old would have been well pleased with what had risen out of the barren ground. Had someone come along and created an illustration of the cathedral, it would have fit well in the pages of the book he had treasured for the entirety of his life. Above his head an achievement of miraculous proportions rose into the sky. God placed a dream in his heart, and he had sacrificed everything to pursue it. And yet, he felt little in the way of accomplishment. What he gave, no one wanted. In the eyes of the common man, the cathedral was a thing to be captured. He felt tired. His body longed for death.

Adeo stacked the gold into a basket.

"What now?" asked Rafa.

"Tonight, we finish."

They hauled the gold load by load to the tower and there placed it for the final crowning. He worked without ceasing until the shape of mother and child appeared in a cast of gold. The metal sizzled in the mold and turned black with heat. The liquified gold needed to cool and harden before he could raise the statue and polish the exterior into its full glory.

Before dawn, torches appeared on the horizon. Men assembled and marched through the pass intending to find Adeo and kill him. They had justification for vengeance. Brothers and fathers and husbands had been slain. They demanded his blood as payment.

"Protect me," Adeo prayed to God.

"You have nothing to fear," God said to him. "I will finish what I started in you."

A storm swirled overhead and sent a sheet of rain onto the earth below. The torches extinguished, but the men marched on. Lightning ripped across the sky and lit the valley. Hundreds from the town came his way, some on horseback and some on foot.

Lightning struck again, and on the western horizon he saw Sufiya and her warriors riding at full speed to meet them.

"To introduce something beautiful into the world is to start a war. Over and over again, I have seen it," Rafa said. "Christ did not come to bring peace, but the sword. You would be wise to remember that. Nothing is for everyone. Especially not a place like this."

The two armies moved towards the cathedral like a meeting of tides. The winner would take the church as their prize. Lightning struck once more and he saw Sufiya leading her warriors. She rode with her head low against the horse's neck and there she whispered the ancient language learned from the desert and with these words the horse ran faster than the rest. She drew her sword and held it behind her as a rudder in the wind.

Lightning struck and the sky held the splintering arms of white and blue as if in a bowl. The lightning fought to strike once more but the sky made it wait and in the prolonged waiting the tension grew stronger and stronger. Adeo placed his hands on the metal cast and found it had cooled enough to lift. Rafa helped him pick up the statue and shift it into place on the landing. The mother held her child. She looked over the desert below and all the world looked up at her. The cathedral had been crowned in a symbol of peace.

The sky with all its might held back the lightning as time came to a standstill.

The armies stopped their pursuit in awe of the luminous mother presiding over the desert. She carried the child in her arms and the Spirit of God in her soul. The kingdom of earth and the kingdom of heaven met in the sacred individual, the one who lived in remembrance, and this she symbolized in full.

A blaze of golden light slowly spread from the statue and then pierced the dark as the sun broke over the horizon.

The beam of gold hit Sufiya's face first.

The pain started in her eyes but moved to her face and seized upon the scar. She pulled her horse to a stop and dismounted. She removed both hat and mask and tried to cover herself from the light but could not do so. The light pressed through her skin. It indwelled her. She felt the scar on her cheek burning and then disappearing. New skin formed where once the slash of a razor had left her disfigured. With no other recourse she opened her eyes and faced the light head on. She soon understood she was not being destroyed but rather renewed from within and in this truth she cast her sword aside.

The cathedral had been finished.

The strange boy she met long ago in the hidden places of the desert had done what he set out to do.

In the flood of golden light she saw a shape coming towards her. Her vision narrowed into a tunnel and at the end of it stood The Horse, not as she had seen him last but as she had seen him that day in the street. Once more she was like the child reaching out her hand to touch a beautiful and wild thing.

"I know your name," she said.

* * *

On the other plain the army of men came to a standstill.

They, too, were paralyzed by the wonder of light. The golden crown of the cathedral filled their eyes with a glory they did not recognize. It came from a place beyond their memories or imaginations. They stood in silence and resisted the urge to shield themselves from the revelation. They cast their weapons aside, for before them was displayed a divine power that could not be won through the violence of men.

If only for a moment, they remembered.

* * *

And then, the sky could hold back the lightning no longer.

A strike of pure light pierced through the statue and shook the earth. The bolt tore through the roof and dragged across the floor until it landed on the center of the altar.

Adeo entered a universe of white as the cathedral erupted in flames.

* * *

He awoke at midday on the desert floor.

He coughed the sand out of his mouth and wiped it from his tongue. When doing so he felt the blood sticky on the cracks of his lips. To open his eyes was a struggle not only because of the blinding sun but because his skin was burned from lying exposed for days on end. He knew not how long he had been here and shielded his eyes as he sat up.

The cathedral was destroyed.

The pieces once assembled in order and beauty had been reduced to their origin state. The world had been wiped flat. The table upon which the cathedral was built had been shaken. The structure collapsed. The glass shattered. Everyone was gone. All that once lived in this place was either dead or had fled for safety in the terror of the storm. The tents and fences and markings of men lay buried unseen beneath sweeps of sand, and there they would deteriorate into nothingness over the centuries to come. The desert had reclaimed the space as its own.

Smoke rose from the remains of the cathedral.

"Rafa?" Adeo said quietly. "Where are you?"

The words barely left his mouth.

In the corpse of the cathedral he saw no glass, no statues, no works formed by his own hand. He saw only stone and sand and hot smoke rising out of the cracks. The pile of stones reached high into the sky in a triangular shape. The tower and spires had fallen inward and collapsed together. And yet, somehow the stone had settled so that a doorway formed at the base that looked much like the entrance to La Catedral.

Inside the mountain of stone Adeo heard someone singing.

"Rafa?" he asked again, louder now.

Adeo stood up with difficulty.

In the doorway a shape materialized. The singing came to a stop.

"You're alive," said the voice.

The figure moved into the light.

She had grown old but he recognized her at once. She still carried the beauty of her youth. She wore a dress of flowing white and leaned against the stone. He moved one step towards her and then another.

"Zelie," he said.

"Adeo."

"Where are we?" Adeo asked.

"Together," she said. "At last."

"Are we alive?"

Zelie laughed. "One of us, yes. The other, barely."

Adeo looked at his own hands. He pressed his thumbs into his palms to feel the flesh and bone.

"How did you find me?"

She wished to say much but said little.

"With great difficulty," she said. She ran her hands over the smoothed edges of stone. "It must have been beautiful. I can imagine it. Just like the drawings in your notebook."

"Nothing happened as I thought it would," he said.

Zelie smiled. She moved towards him. "Nothing happened as I thought it would, either. And that is ok. I lived an entire life apart from you. A beautiful life. But I discovered that we cannot hold on to the things we love. When the time comes for them to go, you must let them go."

Adeo nodded.

"That day I saw you in the church. In your dress. You looked happy."

"I was. It was the happiest day of my life," she said. "You looked happy, too. Holding your bucket and your hammer."

"I was dreaming of this. All of this," he said. He motioned to the destroyed cathedral. "But I did not know what it would cost. How could I have known?"

At her feet she brushed aside sand to reveal part of a shattered statue.

"I saw you coming to me," Adeo said. "Years ago. In dreams."

She smiled. "And I saw you, too. You and your great cathedral in the desert. My God. Look at you. I prayed for you. So many nights. My children prayed for you," Zelie said. "They did not know you, but they believed a man on the other side of the world was building a cathedral on his own. I wrote stories about you. They found them so funny, and so wonderful, and so inspiring. And they prayed for you. They thought you were a crazy man. But now they tell the stories to their own children. I think each time the cathedral gets bigger and bigger."

For the first time in many years, he laughed.

Adeo looked past her at the mountain of unformed stones. He had no money. He had no children. He had no glory. He had no fame. He had no power to wield. He no longer had the promise of youth or the strength to lift another stone. He was an old man dying slowly in the desert, and the cathedral he spent a lifetime building was destroyed.

And yet, somehow, it was complete.

"Tell me what it was like," Zelie said. She looked into Adeo's eyes. "Describe it to me. In every detail. The cathedral I saw in my dreams."

"You are seeing it now," Adeo said. "Wherever I go, there it will be."

To discover more of my work, visit:
craigscunningham.com

www.ingramcontent.com/pod-product-compliance
Lightning Source LLC
LaVergne TN
LVHW051014080826
845145LV00009B/2617

9781967262472